THE RYDER BRAND

Jack Ryder had had enough of killing in the Civil War and, indeed, had barely survived. Now, working as an attorney, he'd come out West for a quiet life. However, Dutton Mazer, whose family own the biggest spread thereabouts, picks a fight with Jack. Then his father, Bull Mazer, tries to take over the entire range by resorting to kidnapping and arson . . . But when they stoop to murder, Jack must pin on a star and fight fire with fire, bullet with bullet . . .

*Books by Mike Stall
in the Linford Western Library:*

GUN AND STAR
THE SPUR LINE
THE HIDDEN APACHES
WEST OF EDEN

MIKE STALL

THE RYDER BRAND

Complete and Unabridged

LINFORD
Leicester

First published in Great Britain in 2005 by
Robert Hale Limited

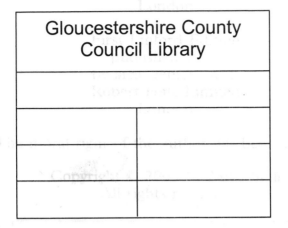

Stall, Mike
    The Ryder brand.—Large print ed.—
Linford western library
1. Western stories
2. Large type books
I. Title
823.9'14 [F]

    ISBN 1–84617–356–6

Published by
F. A. Thorpe (Publishing)
Anstey, Leicestershire

Set by Words & Graphics Ltd.
Anstey, Leicestershire
Printed and bound in Great Britain by
T. J. International Ltd., Padstow, Cornwall

This book is printed on acid-free paper

Prologue

Jack Ryder badly wanted a cigar but he could hardly light up and risk offending the rather pretty young lady seated beside him. Unlike back east there weren't any smoking compartments on the train; gentlemen were supposed to step outside onto the platform and enjoy their vice in the open air. But then he'd have to get up, fiddle with his walking stick and see the pity in her eyes.

Of course, there might be none there. Her prettiness had a rather vacuous, self regarding quality to it and she probably wouldn't think about him either way, but it didn't matter. He'd do without. They were only half an hour from Tamar City if the schedule could be believed.

He tried to content himself by looking out of the window but nothing

1

had changed, just flat, sparsely-grassed land with a hint of mountains way to the north. Cattle country. Except he'd seen very few so far. Probably they didn't like the noise and avoided the area, though it could just be the sheer size of the land. Even back east the distances weren't small but out here the land just seemed to go on forever. He already felt as if he'd been born on a train and only the assurance of the schedule stopped him from believing he'd die on one.

'You don't mind, do you?'

Ryder looked to the girl beside him. She was holding one of those new fangled pre-rolled cigarettes with every intention of smoking it.

'No, of course not,' he said quickly, suppressing a smile. 'Let me light it for you, ma'am.' He delved into the pocket of his jacket and brought forth a pack of lucifers.

'Thanks,' she said, drawing deeply on the cigarette. 'I was going nuts for that.'

'You were?' Ryder said, for want of anything better.

'Sure, I know some men don't approve but I am an artiste after all.'

He must have looked a question because she added: 'Rebecca de Morphe, singer and dancer.' She held out her free hand. He took it.

'Jack Ryder. I'm an attorney.'

'Pleased to meet you, Jack. I hope I'll see you at the Tamar City Opera House — and you can see me.'

'Surely,' he said, not quite sure what 'seeing' her meant. 'Artiste' could cover a lot of ground. He noticed now the slightly too frilly nature of her dress, the strength of the perfume, the perhaps excessive touches of rouge on her cheeks. But he didn't jump to conclusions. She might just be a singer and dancer and no more.

'Light up yourself. If you care to,' she said.

'Thanks, ma'am, but I think I'll wait,' he said. The urge had gone completely.

★ ★ ★

The train was exactly on time. Suddenly they were slowing up before sidings lined with cattle pens, all empty. The buildings of the town, what little he saw of them before the train stopped at the depot, were all balloon style — wooden, made of thousands of two-by-fours and tens of thousands of nails.

'Nice meeting you,' Rebecca de Morphe said, getting up.

'And you, ma'am,' he replied, levering himself up just slightly: the netted baggage rack immediately above him giving him a welcome excuse not to stand fully.

He watched her leave, seeing even more frills behind than before, and then she was lost in the crowd of departing passengers.

Ryder just sat there. There was no haste. This was a single track spur line that went no further, yet. This was, for the moment, the back of beyond. Which was why he was here. He'd wanted to make a new beginning.

He extricated the stick from between himself and the window. There was nothing fancy about it, a stout ashen staff suitable for an old man or cripple. He paused a moment then used it to lever himself erect.

After so many hours of sitting the pain in his lower right leg was horrible, but he was used to that. All the same, it suggested not so much a new beginning as a continuation of things as before.

He braced himself against the seat a moment, scarcely thinking, and took the stick in both hands. All the pent up fury in him was suddenly in his hands and the crack of the breaking stick rung out like a shot.

A moment later a uniformed railroad man entered the carriage. 'Are you OK, sir?'

'Fine,' Ryder said, tossing the remains of the walking stick onto the seat. 'I've nothing here but my trunk — '

'That'll be taken care of, sir.'

'Thanks,' Ryder said and was glad to see him go, it would be easier if no one saw him start moving.

It was bad, the jar from breaking the stick seemed to have gone down into his knee and calf and he was tempted to use the seats for support but outside the carriage there would be no such luxury. He persevered, walking slowly, perhaps limping a little but, so he judged, not extravagantly. It hurt like hell but he also found he just didn't care.

After all, this was a new beginning.

Part One

1

The Tamar Hotel really was just that and not a glorified bar: it had rooms in abundance. Ryder saw the room keys hanging on the wall behind the reception desk, most with an undisturbed look to them. The spare capacity presumably was for the odd times when hordes of cattle buyers descended on the town demanding somewhere to stay. Presumably the prices went up dramatically too, though in all truth the dollar a night he was paying was still somewhat exorbitant. The room turned out to be small, the bed hard and the kerosene lamp dim. But not so dim that he couldn't see the pint bottle of rye he'd set on the bedside table.

It was a tempting prospect. The ache in his leg was now bearable — he'd borne infinitely worse — but it was still stopping him from sleeping. Ryder wasn't by nature a drinker; occasionally he imbibed for social reasons, and now it seemed perfectly reasonable to take a snort of whiskey to get to sleep. But there was more than reason involved. He doubted anyone was a born drinker; they all started for some reasonable, or at least explainable, cause. The difficulty was in stopping. And he had troubles enough without becoming a drunk.

He sighed and was about to turn down the lamp when he heard the commotion in the corridor outside — shouts, doors banging and odd, assorted noises. Until then it had been as silent as death on this floor. He'd thought there was no one else on it.

Leave it be, he told himself, but one of the voices had sounded feminine — and in trouble. He got ponderously to his feet, pulled his trousers back on and limped barefooted to the door, pausing there a moment in the hope the commotion would subside and die.

It didn't. The female voice started

screaming; there was a thud and now a man's voice was raised. Ryder opened the door.

And was sorry he had. The picture in front of him was very easy to interpret — a half dressed woman was sitting on the floor of the corridor between two men, both obviously cowboys. She was holding her head but no one had hit her; her painted face — powdered, rouged and lips rouged too — was untouched. She'd just been pushed down, out of the way in a drunken brawl between two admirers, though perhaps 'patrons' would be the better word.

Ryder would have closed his door and gone back into his room if the nearer of the two cowboys hadn't gone for his gun. Forgetting the ache in his leg he stepped forward and caught hold of the hand holding the drawn pistol, fixing both in his grasp.

The cowboy turned to him, ready to strike at him with his other hand. Knowing he couldn't stand up in that

11

kind of a fight, Ryder squeezed.

He had never been a weak man, he'd been able to straighten a horse shoe at eighteen, and the years of riding and then handling a pair of crutches had added to that. The cowboy yelped.

Carefully, keeping his thumb over the hammer, he took the gun from the man's hand. It was easy: the other no longer cared to keep it, grasping his right hand with his left when it was free as if to check the fingers were still attached.

It wasn't necessary, Ryder knew. He'd broken no bones; it just felt as if he had. He looked to the woman. 'Ma'am, you'd best be about your business,' not realising until he'd said the words that they could be construed as encouraging vice.

'Get him, Billy!' the hurt man said and Ryder realized that the enemies of moments before had reverted to what they always were — buddies.

He'd been a damned fool to get involved, but you couldn't stand by and see murder done, even if you were only barely able to stand.

Billy, the one addressed, made a tentative motion towards his gun. The gun in Ryder's hand was cocked and pointed in an instant and Billy's interest in drawing his own died. A moment later the object of their rival attentions picked herself up off the floor and vanished into one of the rooms, slamming the door behind her and then sending the bolt home with a resounding crack.

'You bastard!' the man with the injured hand raved, staring at him, eyes wet with tears of pain and rage. 'I'll get you for — '

'You'll get yourself gone,' Ryder said softly — a man with a cocked gun in his hand had no need to shout — 'and you'll sleep it off. You can collect your gun from the desk clerk in the morning.'

'You don't know who you're dealing with, you — '

'I don't take too kindly to insults,

whoever you are. I'll excuse the one because you were hurting but my patience is limited. Get going before you get hurt more. You too, Billy.'

Ryder could see the hatred in the other's eyes, and his face. It was quite a handsome face, a little on the fleshy side but not excessively so. It was also very much the face of a man used to getting his own way.

But not this time. Now he daren't even speak for fear of those terrible hands or that cocked gun. All he could do was hesitate a long moment radiating impotent rage, then turn and move down the corridor. Billy put a hand out to him; he shrugged it away; and then both were gone.

Ryder stood there a moment, not anxious to test his leg, and then he realized that if he lingered too long the object of the dispute might well reappear having decided that to the victor belonged the spoils.

He went back into his room as quickly as he could, barring his own door this time. She mightn't be put off by a cocked pistol . . .

He sat on the bed and for want of anything better to do he examined the pistol he'd taken off the drunken cowboy. It was one of the famous Colt Frontier pistols, still single action but with cartridges. The revolvers he'd been used to during the war had been cap and ball but this had a nice balance to it and the way the cartridges went in through the gate was ingenious.

He set it on the table and lay back on the bed, not even bothering to take off his trousers again. He'd been stupid enough to involve himself in an argument between two drunken cowboys over the favours of a drab; it was hardly an auspicious start to his self-proclaimed new beginning. But he found he didn't care. He'd been in the right and he'd done his duty.

2

'I'm sorry I couldn't be here to meet you yesterday,' Lawyer Bridger said, leaning back in his chair. His ample stomach was still only inches off the edge of his desk. 'It's not like back east, say in Philadelphia or New York. There the business all comes to the office. Out here, oftentimes we have to go to it.'

'I'm hardly a Philadelphia lawyer, sir,' Ryder said.

Bridger smiled. 'Heck, I'm not ever likely to plead before the Supreme Court myself. But why come all this way to start practising law? From what I hear, you were well thought of back home.'

Ryder shrugged. 'I fancied the far horizons.'

Bridger smiled again. 'I can't argue with that as I once did myself. But I can tell you this — the horizon never gets any closer.'

'If only I'd known earlier.'

Bridger chuckled. 'You'll do, Ryder. Hell, you don't mind if I call you Jack? Call me Stoney by the way, everybody does. Stone bridge, eh? I reckon it could have been worse. I could have been re-christened 'Humpback'.'

'Or 'Toll'.'

'That's quick for a lawyer out here, Jack. Most of 'em have no sense of humour either. I reckon we've chosen the wrong profession.'

'Speaking of which, what about the state bar?'

'You can forget more examinations. We haven't been a state all that long and we're not so formal whatever it says on paper. It just takes one state court to admit you and you can practise in all. Considering that I was asked to take you on by Judge Shaw, I don't reckon he'll exactly object to you.' He paused, then: 'Can you ride?'

Ryder was taken aback for all it was

an obvious question.

'It's that right leg that pains you, ain't it?' Bridger persisted.

'Yes.'

'No problem then, we get on horses from the left out west.'

'And back east too, sir.'

'Stoney.'

'Then I can ride, Stoney,' Ryder said, deciding. He hadn't been on a horse in years but then this was a new beginning.

'And shoot?'

'If I have to,' Ryder said, 'but I thought I was here to plead cases?'

'So did I but then I heard tell you'd had a run in with young Dutton Mazer.' He paused and smiled. 'It's a small town.'

'And it's already thinking me a fool for getting involved with drunken riffraff.'

Suddenly Bridger was very serious. 'No, your reputation went up with nine tenths of the population of Tamar City. That young gentleman — your description is appropriate but isn't much used as his father owns the biggest spread around — is heartily disliked. And feared.'

'He wasn't all that fearsome last night.'

'I heard you trapped his hand in a door.'

'I just prised a gun out of it. He should have it back by now. I left it for him at the hotel desk.'

Bridger laughed, shortly. 'Hell, I bet he enjoyed collecting it.'

'Do you think it'll be a problem?'

'I reckon not. You don't wear a gun nor can you be expected to, being a lawyer. And his pa knows you're some kind of kin to Judge Shaw.'

'He's just a family friend.'

'Don't tell anyone. You'll be safer that way and the rumour will do our business no harm at all. Still, keep out of dark alleys for a while!'

3

It had been a bad night and the pint of rye was now half gone. But as he walked towards the court house, Ryder found his leg less troublesome than expected. Maybe he should have thrown that stick away a year ago.

He came to the edge of the wooden sidewalk and used a hitching rail to swing himself up onto it. There was no horse to disturb and scarcely anyone about. Tamar City seemed almost abandoned, a bunch of cheap wooden buildings planted in a great plain of grass for no good reason. Except there was a reason — cattle. The city serviced the ranches, sold their cattle, penned them and shipped them out. But not now, at this precise moment. For now, it was just waiting.

The court house was next door to the county sheriff's office, doubtless a planned convenience, and Ryder entered to find Bridger already there. He was seated behind the left-hand-side lawyers' table. The judge's raised platform and desk were unoccupied. There was no one on the prosecution side and only a couple of spectators at the back — old men with nothing else to do. The mayor, whose court this currently was, hadn't arrived yet.

'Sit down,' Bridger said. 'Mayor Jackman's always late.'

Ryder eased himself onto the chair. 'Who are we representing?'

'Probably no one. Jackman holds his court at least once a week even if only to adjourn it for lack of business. I like to attend, it's good business, but in future this will be your job.'

Ryder had a lot of questions but he thought it better to keep them to himself. At last the mayor arrived. They stood up briefly. Jackman was a smallish man in a dark, serge suit. He lit a cigar as soon as he ensconced himself and so did Bridger. Ryder didn't.

'Bring 'em in,' Jackson shouted. A door to the left opened and a small procession of malefactors entered. They looked hungover rather than overawed by the proceedings and the man following them, a grizzled oldster wearing a deputy sheriff's badge, wasn't even wearing a gun.

'What have you got for us, Tommy?' Jackman asked.

'Three cases of drunk and disorderly, Mr Mayor,' the oldster said.

'And the sheriff?'

'Not available, Mr Mayor. He told me to lay charges for him.'

Jackman sighed. 'I assume you'll be giving evidence against 'em, too, Deputy Gill?'

'Sure thing.'

'Attorney Bridger, will you undertake the prosecution? We can't have Tommy Gill prosecuting and giving evidence.'

'Happy to, Mr Mayor.' Bridger motioned the three accused to approach his table.

'Any dispute about the charge?' he 'whispered' in a voice that could still be heard around the court.

The first of the three shook his head; the second shrugged; and the third, who looked a tad less disreputable than his fellows, said: 'I guess I took one over the odds, Mr Bridger. I can't remember much about it.'

'Right,' Bridger said and waved them to the side. Then he stood up. 'Mr Mayor, acting for the sheriff I lay charges against all three — of being drunk and causing disorder. They all plead guilty. As usual, Harries and Donachy throw themselves upon the mercy of the court and Mr Wilson offers his apologies. As the court knows, he's employed in the livery and is a hard-working citizen. On this occasion he allowed the drink to take him over, it being the anniversary of a private sorrow. He solemnly promises that it will never happen again.'

The mayor nodded and spoke: 'As for Harries and Donachy, a severe admonition from the court and a fine of five dollars or ten days in the county jail, at the sheriff's discretion.' He paused and looked hard at the third miscreant. 'Mr Wilson, I haven't seen you here for some time and I don't want to see you here again. You are discharged.'

The deputy nodded to the mayor and led off his little procession — back through the same door they had come in by, all except for Wilson — now a free man — who left by the front door.

'That seems to take care of business, Stoney,' the mayor said. 'Now you can introduce your new associate.' He left the podium, came down and offered his hand. Ryder took it, gently.

'So what did you think of our little court?' Jackman asked. 'Did it strike you as irregular?'

It had — Bridger had combined the roles of prosecutor and defence counsel in a way which would have got him disbarred back east. Jackman too had been very light on formality. But Ryder also knew he was being taught a lesson, and the thing to do was to learn it.

'It struck me as practical, Mr Mayor. I guess the first two were the town drunks who presumably didn't have the money to pay a fine, and by making the period of incarceration at the sheriff's discretion you allow him to toss them out if he needs the cells. As for Wilson, he has a job but currently no money. If you'd jailed him he'd have lost his job and the town a good liveryman, which I presume he is.'

Jackman laughed. 'And I thought we'd a tenderfoot on our hands, Stoney — unless you've been coaching him?'

'No, he worked it out on his own. I wanted to see if he could and he not only could, he did.'

'You'll fit in well here, Ryder,' the mayor said. 'I'm damned glad we've got you.'

★   ★   ★

'You missed some of it,' Bridger said when they were walking back to the office. The fat man was naturally taking his time and Ryder had no difficulty keeping pace. 'For instance, the sheriff'll throw those bums out as soon as he gets back from wherever. The only reason they were charged is because Tommy Gill gets six bits for every arrest that's brought to court and Mayor Jackson likes to play judge.'

'So why were we there?'

'For the six dollars — two dollars each for prosecuting. It's easy money. The practice makes much more on the civil side but everything's grist to the old mill.' He paused. 'You did well, Jack. Jackman meant what he said. He's our banker too so it's a double score. I didn't guess you'd — '

'Good morning, Mr Ryder. And you too, sir.'

They both stopped, tipped their hats to Miss de Morphe who was before them on the sidewalk. She was wearing a green velvet dress with a large bustle, the whole adorned with purple flowers. It was cut low at the breasts and had

26

puffed sleeves. Worse, Ryder saw her face now had more than just a hint of rouge; it was painted and powdered, her eyelashes were darkened with kohl and her lips rouged. Her profession was quite obvious.

'Ma'am,' Bridger said.

'Good morning, ma'am,' Ryder said.

'It's good to see you again, Mr Ryder, and to be able to thank you. All the ladies of Tamar City feel safer knowing there are gentlemen like you about.'

'I'm obliged, ma'am,' Ryder said, realizing that the ladies in question were that by courtesy only.

'Au revoir, gentlemen,' she said and flounced past. Ryder could see Bridger was having difficulty in keeping a straight face

'We met on the train,' Ryder said, somewhat lamely.

'No doubt.'

'She said she was a singer and a dancer,' Ryder said. 'I'm sorry it was a euphemism.' He meant it too: she was somebody's sister, somebody's daughter, and he guessed she'd been pretty even before she'd taken to wearing all that paint.

'I doubt the local cowboys will agree,' Bridger said.

Nor Bridger himself, Ryder guessed, but said nothing.

4

Dutton Mazer dismounted, favouring his right hand, and tethered his horse to a bush before walking down slope towards the centre of the depression. It was a tangle of vegetation; cattle often got in difficulties here but there were none evident now, just the old cotton-wood at its centre. He stopped twenty yards from the tree and stood facing it, letting his bandaged hand hang just over his holstered Colt.

He drew but didn't fire — his thumb refused to cock the Colt and his crushed fingers could barely hold it. He sobbed aloud in misery and self pity — that lousy bastard had done this to him!

He took the gun with his uninjured left hand and started walking towards the tree, firing as he went. His first two shots missed but the next four hit, sending bark flying in a satisfactory manner. But slow, too slow! He'd had to pause and cock the gun each time, nothing like the smooth motion he could manage with his right.

He stood there, the gun hanging down to his left, his right hand cradled across his chest, and let the tears flow. Humiliated and injured and nobody cared. His pa, old Bull Mazer, had told him he was a damned fool fighting over whores, and Doc Bluett had said the injury was minor, nothing broken, not even a torn tendon, just crushed muscles. It would get better but it would take time.

Yet in the meantime he was a cripple, forced to ride out here alone into this place so no one would hear him practising — and failing miserably. He'd always been the fastest draw on the ranch, in the whole region. The name Dutton Mazer had meant something, nobody crossed him, ever. Now, any of the hands on the ranch could call him out and beat him.

Even Billy Wendt, and he wouldn't forget that it had all started with him, though he'd let him keep thinking he'd forgiven and forgotten. But it had been Billy who'd crossed him over that bitch Donna. Oh, how she'd pay too! But both of them would wait. Billy had been on the Mazer spread these ten years now and thought he belonged. He didn't. Donna — No, she came last. First and above all he had to deal with that incomer, that lawman — Jack Ryder.

He shuddered, remembering. The strength of the man was incredible. He didn't look much either, taller than average maybe but not so tall as his pa, Bull Mazer, and not muscled like him either, but the strength of those hands was something even Bull couldn't match. And the way he'd handled a gun suggested he knew what he was doing there too.

No, he wasn't someone to approach straight on. He didn't deserve a chance. He hadn't given him one.

Dutton Mazer reholstered the Colt with difficulty; his hand still ached like crazy. Then he turned and walked back the way he had come, wiping his eyes as he went.

He knew now what he would do. He had to put up a front, even make a joke of it all. Yes, that would keep Billy Wendt happy and he needed that — the last thing he wanted was for Billy to leave.

His pa had always counselled him to patience. He who waits, gets. Well, he'd wait but only until his poor torn hand had healed, and maybe not even that long.

He found his horse waiting patiently, hurt his hand again as he mounted and, as if in revenge, dug his rowelled spurs deep into the beast's flanks.

Part Two

1

Sheriff Mason was a notably straight-laced man. He had a large property to the south of the railroad — where the land merged into desert — and perhaps some of the dryness of the land had got into his soul. Still he enforced the law without fear or favour and kept the cost down too — he had no interest in filling up his jail with petty offenders just for the sake of it, and even he didn't object to a certain degree of rowdiness on Saturday nights, provided it was kept strictly in its place. The fact that all the saloons employed 'waitresses' who did rather more than wait table and serve drinks might not be strictly legal but it didn't worry him — it was old custom. But it had to be kept in its place, and that was mostly out of sight.

Donna Biddable, Miss de Morphe and Aimée Teaze had walked down

35

Main Street arm in arm on the way to the dress shop and in rather too high spirits. So he had arrested them and locked them up in the county jail.

'You see to it,' Bridger said to Ryder when the proprietor of the Opera House came to the office to hire their services, 'it seems to be your speciality.' He was smiling a little and so was the saloon keeper, the latter a little uncertainly knowing that Ryder had not frequented his premises so far, not even just to drink.

Ryder looked him over, unconcerned. He was a small, seedy looking man in a too fancy suit and with a hint of scent about him. But Bridger needed to be shown his new associate couldn't be pushed around.

'Right,' he said, 'I'll plead 'em guilty and throw them on the mercy of the court. Probably a twenty five dollar fine, time served and an admonition as to their future conduct. The hearing will be tomorrow.'

'Hell,' the little man said — his name

was Skinner — 'I don't care about the money but they'll kill me if they have to spend a night in jail.' He looked worried. So that was the way things were at the Opera House, Ryder thought, surprised, and then he realized that women were at a premium out here. Skinner couldn't play the traditional pimp.

'Maybe I can get them off without going to court,' Ryder said, 'but the fee will be same as the fines.'

'Twenty five bucks is fine.'

'A piece.'

Skinner hesitated, then shrugged. 'If you can do it.'

'I can,' Ryder said committing himself and realizing he was going to look a complete fool if he failed. Skinner believed him, he could see, but Bridger was looking rather quizzical. As well he might, Ryder thought, for he didn't have the slightest idea how he was going to do it.

★ ★ ★

37

'Hell,' Sheriff Mason said, 'I didn't particularly like arresting 'em, but it had to be done. I've got to keep up standards.'

Looking at him, Ryder had an odd feeling that he was looking at himself in twenty years time. He pushed the thought aside. 'I agree,' he said pausing briefly, then added 'you know we're representing them in court?'

'I didn't but that's to the good. I'll present the county's case myself.'

'Fine,' Ryder said, 'but as to the nature of the charge — '

'Lewd conduct,' Mason said instantly.

And Ryder knew he had him. If Mason had gone for disorderly conduct, it would have been all up. It was vague enough for any circumstances. But not this.

'I thought so,' Ryder said, 'which is why I came over to have a private word. As I understand it, they didn't specifically make an offer to anyone.'

'We all know what they are.'

'Precisely, but when I cross-examine

you tomorrow you'll have to say that, and by doing so admit publicly they're tolerated in the saloons. Again, everybody knows it but it doesn't look good for a sheriff to have to admit it.'

Mason rubbed his chin. 'Yeah, there is that. Thanks for warning me.'

'I'd prefer not to have to ask that question at all.'

'How?'

'Do we really need to take it to court?'

'I'd look weak if I was talked out of it.'

'Who's to say you were? I know I couldn't do it. But perhaps the point's already made without going to court. Leave them another hour or so then give them a stern warning and boot 'em out. You could even tell them you've had a word with the lawyers and that if it happens again the only defence we'd make for them is to plead them guilty and throw them on the mercy of the court.'

Mason considered the matter for a

moment, then stood up and offered Ryder his hand. 'I'll do that — and I'm obliged. I hadn't foreseen what could happen in court.'

'That's because you're a lawman, sheriff, not a lawyer. You enforce the law and we get in the way.'

'Hell, that's a good 'un, Ryder, I'll remember that.'

He probably would, Ryder thought, he probably would . . .

⋆　⋆　⋆

'You'd really have pressed him about tolerating saloon girls in open court?' Bridger asked when they were alone in the office.

'I might have,' Ryder said. 'Or I might have suggested charging them with disorderly conduct just before he preferred charges. I don't reckon Mayor Jackman would have gone against the sheriff however I'd presented the case. But this was everybody wins — we do, the girls don't spend a night in jail and

Mason keeps his dignity intact.'

Bridger laughed. 'You're trickier than I thought, Jack, and you learn fast. But as you say, nobody loses and that's important out here. In a few years I suppose we'll all be as formal as Philadelphia, following every jot and tittle of the regulations, but not yet. Not unless it really counts.'

'You thought I'd make a fool of myself with the case,' Ryder said.

'Yep, I did, and I was wrong. It doesn't do a young lawyer any harm to do that occasionally, but then you're not quite the usual young lawyer.'

'I'm not that young.'

'Yeah, the war took a few years out of most people's lives back east.' He paused as if to let Ryder continue.

Ryder didn't. The war was the last thing he wanted to talk about.

2

In just a few weeks Ryder got to know Tamar City pretty well. He'd had a picture of the west in his mind before he came — the men all wearing six-guns, plenty of blue-eyed damsels in need of rescuing, mighty herds of cattle, mightier deeds to be done. Aside from the six-guns — which were common enough — the dime-novel picture hadn't quite worked out. Cows were rarely seen save after round up, excepting a few specimens delivered to the local abattoir; the ranchers made only occasional appearances in town and their daughters, when they accompanied them, were neither in obvious need of rescue nor particularly appealing. They had a hearty look to them. So far, his knightly deeds had amounted to writing wills and pleading out the odd misdemeanour before the mayor, the city's only and ex-officio magistrate. Shaw, the circuit judge, was due any time now but wouldn't stay long as there were no felonies for him to try.

There were legal disputes, about land titles, but Bridger sensibly kept these to himself. Technically, Ryder hadn't been accepted as an attorney in the state yet; that was for the judge to do, but no one seemed to care. Bridger assured him he had gained a certain popularity among the young 'ladies' of the Opera House but he'd still left that unvisited. There was just too much temptation there of the liquid kind. The pint bottle in his bedroom still had an inch in it and he intended to keep it that way. Sometimes at night his leg ached like the devil. It hurt less during the day now but enough to keep him walking slowly and grim faced. If he were to let himself limp it might well hurt less and nobody would care, but he did. Better to be thought a cold fish than show weakness. That was one of the reasons he'd come west. Back home they all knew him and would make allowances. Not here.

But he still had to get to know the land, and the only way to do that was on horseback. So one Saturday morning he walked, slowly, towards the livery, occasionally tipping his hat to new acquaintances and generally doing his best to hide his anxiety.

'Hi, Mr Ryder,' Wilson said when he entered the livery stables.

Ryder returned the greeting, then said, 'I need a horse.'

'You're taking out Mr Bridger's buggy? By the way, I'm grateful to both of you for getting me off back then. I'm not normally a drinking man, you understand, but occasionally I get a yen for it.'

'That was down to Mr Bridger,' Ryder said.

'Still, I'm grateful. Want me to fix up the buggy?'

'I'll ride.'

'Right, sir. I've a nice little gelding — '

'I'll pick my own, if I may.'

'You know horses?'

'A little,' Ryder said, unsmiling. For

some reason his leg had begun to pain him, abominably. He set his face and walked past the stalls, stopping before a bay.

'Yeah, I reckon you do,' Wilson said. 'I'll saddle her for you.'

Ryder nodded, waiting for the ordeal of mounting up, but when Wilson had completed his task the liveryman said: 'Just a minute, Mr Ryder, there's something Mr Bridger asked me to make sure of.' He walked over to the buggy, found what looked like a bundle of old clothes and extracted a gunbelt from it, which he presented to Ryder.

It had a fine holster and Ryder pulled out a cap and ball pistol. He let it slide back. 'When was it last used?'

Wilson shrugged.

Ryder wasn't about to strap on a cap and ball pistol of that age, which might well have had the delicate caps in place for years. There was another problem which he demonstrated. He extended the belt, having to stretch his arms to do it.

Wilson laughed. 'Give it here, sir,' he

said and took it into the little office cubicle to the side, emerging a moment later with a rather more serviceable modern Colt in an open holstered belt with ammunition in the loops. Ryder strapped it on.

'Mr Bridger said not to let you go anywhere without a gun. Nobody does.'

Ryder didn't ask why. 'How much do I owe you?'

Wilson shook his head. 'It's on Mr Bridger's account. Except the gun. If you want to get some practice in you can pay for the ammunition when you get back.'

'I might do that,' Ryder said. 'I'm obliged.'

It was now time to mount up. He checked the cinch, then grasped the cantle and set his left foot in the stirrup, putting all his weight on his right leg. It hurt like the devil for an instant, then he swung himself into the saddle.

He breathed out gently. He was home.

3

Close up, the land was by no means as featureless as it had appeared from the train — there were numerous dips and depressions, and low knolls too. There was no barbed wire either, not in these parts: the boundary between the Thornton and Mazer ranches was the river. Provided he kept south of it he would avoid Dutton Mazer just as he did by avoiding dark alleys in town.

He'd met Chan Thornton in town. He was a tall, rangy man, slow speaking but of good disposition. He'd invited him to ride out to his ranch at any time and on his range at pleasure. Why not? Thornton had nothing to fear from lawyers. Besides, he and Bridger were pretty close. Thornton's spread wasn't as big as Mazer's but just as rich for, according to Bridger, Thornton was the better rancher. He and Mazer were in competition and Bridger reckoned Thornton would win out in the end. Especially when Dutton took over the reins of the Mazer ranch. That at least seemed highly probable: drunks who fight over drabs don't build empires, not even cattle empires. They lose them, fast,

Thornton didn't have a son, just one daughter. Ryder hadn't met her but if she were anything like the rest she'd be a hundred and sixty pounds of muscle and cow-eyed to boot. Pioneers were admirable people, without a doubt, but hardly the most graceful.

The bay edged to the right without instructions via the reins and Ryder, whose mind had momentarily been off riding, looked before he corrected. There was a dip in the land, and a deep one. The vegetation in its centre was thick. The mare was right. There would be pot holes hidden in there: safer to ride its rim.

Ryder halted his horse and considered: there were no cows about to

48

startle, nor people, and if he went down into the dip the sound wouldn't carry very far. And he had to admit to himself he'd an itch to try out the new-fangled cartridge pistol.

He dismounted, clumsily but less painfully than expected. He un-bitted the mare to give her the opportunity to graze, using his lariat to give her more space but tying it firmly to a bush to ensure she didn't run off at the sound of the first shot — it would be a very long walk back.

He moved down into the depression with some care: a pot hole could do him damage too, but finally he was at its deepest point. He looked around for a target. There wasn't much — a stunted bush twenty yards off, a pile of stones at about half that distance. He settled on the latter. He'd seen impromptu pistol-shooting matches at sixty yards, and taken part in some, but it wasn't practical shooting. In action you were lucky if you hit anything at ten yards and the only absolutely sure way was to ram the barrel into someone's chest and pull the trigger. Even then you might get a misfire. But maybe cartridges were different.

He unhitched the tiny strap over the hammer holding the gun safely in its holster and started to draw — and stopped. He'd intended to draw and aim but that wasn't the way they did it out here. You drew, pulled back the hammer while the gun was coming up, firing from the hip. He let the revolver slip back into its holster, tensed his hand and drew.

Crack!

He'd managed to pull back the hammer but he hadn't quite hit the target, just the earth two yards from his foot! He tried again.

It wasn't until his sixth shot that he actually hit the target and even then he wasn't sure it wasn't more down to luck than judgement.

He glanced back at the bay. She was grazing contentedly as if she'd been raised on a battlefield. Enough for now?

It would be a while before he got another chance so why not a little success to build on later? He worked the mechanism, extracting the spent cartridges and refilling the gun from the ammunition in the loops of his belt, marvelling at the ease of the procedure — loading a cap and ball revolver was a time consuming business — and then he slid the gun back into its holster.

Crack!

The first shot hit the stones, within a foot of where he'd been aiming. He fired again and by the time he got to the sixth and final shot he was hitting the stone he aimed at. He seemed to be pretty fast too but he'd nothing to judge against. Having strong, quick hands helped, he guessed, and he wasn't exactly an amateur with pistols —

'Hey, you down there!'

He turned, the empty gun still in his hand. Two shots rang out in quick succession, slamming into the ground in front of him. He tossed the gun aside and looked up.

He was on the rim, holding a Henry rifle and on foot though a small black horse stood untethered a little to the side. He was very slight, with a pale face, and suddenly Ryder realized it wasn't a man at all, it was a girl.

'It wasn't loaded,' he said. 'I'd just fired off six.'

'Who are you?' The carbine didn't move from him.

'Jack Ryder from Tamar City. Mr Thornton invited me to visit his ranch. I was — '

'Oh,' she said and even at this distance Ryder could see the pale face suffuse with colour. She was blushing. He wasn't exactly sure why but he smiled nonetheless.

'I'll come up without the gun.' He started forward, not looking down at the ground but at her, and his foot found the unwanted pot hole. Instantly he was falling and twisting and the pain hit him like a rail-road engine. He heard himself yell but only for an instant. Then nothing at all.

4

Ryder awoke to find himself lying in bed in a darkened room, darkened but not quite dark. Enough light got in through the curtains for him to see the ceiling was higher than his wooden box of a hotel room, and the omnipresent smell of dust was missing. Also, the pillows his head was resting on had a frilly edge. The Tamar City Hotel didn't quite run to that. But more important than anything, the pain was gone.

There was pain, a smarting sort of pain but nothing compared to that he had known. He could feel his right leg under the bedclothes and when he moved it slightly the pain didn't restart. He left it at that. It would be back, he knew, but even a brief surcease was better than nothing. He closed his eyes and the delights of freedom from pain were lost in the oblivion of sleep.

'How are you feeling?'

Ryder opened his eyes and blinked at the light. Doc Bluett was standing by the window having just pulled the curtain off.

'You've been stirring for a while, they tell me. I've got to be leaving and I needed to see you first.'

Ryder's gut tightened, bad news. It must have shown in his face too for Bluett smiled:

'No, you're all there, legs and other vital bits. The only thing missing is this.' He delved into his vest pocket and brought out a small, grey object. He then walked over to the bed and offered it to Ryder.

Finding his arms already outside the sheets, Ryder took it and looked at it. It was metal, case shot by the look of it, not anything fired from a rifle, and not intact. Most of it had been sheared away. 'What is it?'

Bluett shrugged. 'I only know where I

found it. In your leg, but only just.' He paused. 'I heard tell from Stoney you'd been badly hurt once but then I saw you in town walking without a limp, and with a face like granite. Hurt like hell, didn't it?'

'Yeah, but I wasn't shot in the leg. At least, the doctors never thought so. My horse was shot, fell on me and smashed my leg. The bone was broken in several places. The only reason I kept it was that at the field hospital they were practising triage and they set me aside to die. But the other wounds, though bloody, were just superficial and by the time they got to me my leg was healing.' He didn't add how badly they'd set it so it had to be broken again later, or anything of the crutches and the persistent agony.

'Don't blame your doctors too much,' Bluett said. 'I reckon that it came through your horse and into you. It was pressing on a nerve, not directly but via the muscle. If you'd kept on with crutches or a stick it'd still be there now. Just by forcing yourself to walk normally you've been working it out. When you fell down in Gypper's Dip, it was the final straw. It cut the skin from the inside and bled through your trousers. Amanda thought she'd shot you.'

'She didn't,' Ryder said. 'In fact, I'm grateful to her for going and getting help.'

'Not her, she took her horse down into the dip, got you over it somehow and led it back here. She's some girl.'

Ryder didn't disagree but he'd another question: 'And?'

Bluett shrugged. 'It depends on how much the nerve was damaged. Maybe badly, maybe not at all. Get out of bed and see.' He unceremoniously pulled back the sheets. Ryder was pleased to see he was wearing a long nightshirt. He moved himself towards the edge of the bed.

'Get on with it, man!' Bluett said irritably.

Ryder paid him no heed. It wouldn't hurt him. He pulled the nightshirt up so he could see where the slight smarting came from and saw a bandage; it wasn't bloody now. Then he was at the edge of the bed, he eased his legs over, firmly gripped the bedhead and stood up.

The polished wooden floor felt cold to his feet but there was no pain to speak of. He reluctantly released hold of the bedhead and took a step. Again, no pain. He took another.

'Well?' Bluett asked.

'It's OK.'

'Yeah,' Bluett said. 'I thought so. It was the flattish side that was pressed on the muscle that was in turn pressing on the nerve. It just gave you pain but that's done with now.'

'And my leg?'

'Hell of a mess, you'll never make a dancer, but I reckon you'll walk OK, without pain. Until you're old enough for rheumatism.'

Ryder let out his breath. 'Thank you, doctor.'

'Thank the pot hole,' Bluett said.

5

'I'm supposed to say she's resting,' Chan Thornton said as he smoked his pipe and half watched Ryder demolish a T-bone steak. 'Truth is, she's embarrassed, shooting at you like that.'

'She did me a favour,' Ryder said. 'That bit of metal was paining me.' He still didn't like admitting weakness but it was hardly a secret in this house, and it was a past weakness. The absence of pain was still a pure delight to him but he knew nothing was forgotten so quickly as pain. By tomorrow — The heck with tomorrow! He tucked into his steak. It was almost Sunday evening; he'd slept the clock around.

'I reckon she knows that too,' Thornton said. 'She'll come around, though there is one thing.' He hesitated.

'Yes?' Ryder asked, temporarily abstaining from chewing.

'Don't mention you saw her in a pair of pants.'

Ryder almost chuckled. So that was it! And now he remembered her blushing when she discovered he wasn't some outlaw or cattle rustler. Presumably they wouldn't have counted.

'Yeah, she's full growed, eighteen now these last three months, but she hasn't got out much.' Thornton puffed on his pipe. 'My fault. Should have married again after her mother died, but . . . ' He broke off.

Ryder nodded, ignorant of whether Thornton was saying once bitten, twice shy or alluding to how deeply he had loved his wife. It scarcely mattered to him either way.

'Bridger thinks very highly of you, Jack. He says you're a clever lawyer, hard as nails and honest to boot.'

Ryder, who had just finished off his steak and was about to wash it down with strong black coffee, took the compliment in his stride. 'He hasn't made me a partner.'

'Give him time,' Thornton said. 'There are big things happening in this region, very big things. A man could do well for himself here.' He paused. 'You were in the war?'

'Yes,' Ryder said, somewhat shortly.

'A captain, I hear.'

Ryder nodded.

'See much action?'

'Some.'

Chan Thornton smiled. 'You're right, it's over and done with, and thank God for that.' He puffed on his pipe, then added 'But remember, big things are going on — and big opportunities for a man who chooses the right side.' He stood up. 'No need to make your mind up now but remember what I said.'

'Yes, sir.' He would remember, though just what Chan Thornton was talking about he wasn't sure at all, except that it wasn't nonsense. He wasn't that kind of man.

'I'll be going out for a while but I'll see you later,' Thornton added.

'I ought to be getting back — '

'Nonsense. You'll stay the night. Doc said you should. I'll have you taken back in the ranch buggy tomorrow.'

Ryder stood up. 'I'm obliged, sir.'

'Least thing we can do, given we damn near shot you. But I won't apologize for that. I'll leave it to my daughter. She's the one with the hasty rifle.' And with that he left the room.

★   ★   ★

Ryder was pacing the room, still amazed by it all, when Amanda entered. He'd been half-expecting a hoyden, a tomboy, but he couldn't have been more wrong. She was wearing a dark green silk dress, very plain and simple, but she needed no more. Her long, light brown hair, which before had been hidden by a hat, now framed a face that almost took his breath away — not classically beautiful but something more, something he saw in her eyes, indeterminate eyes which could be green, grey or even blue depending on how the light caught them.

He had, expecting the hoyden, intended to raise his hands on her entrance and say something like 'don't shoot!' but all such thoughts flew away.

'Mr Ryder,' she said awkwardly.

'My pleasure, Miss Thornton,' he said with some attempt at suavity.

She smiled. 'And mine, sir.' And he saw a slight blush rise from the whiteness of her throat into her face. 'I hope you'll forgive me, sir.'

'For what?'

'For shooting at you.'

'No, ma'am, I won't forgive you, but I'll thank you profoundly for it.'

The blush had suffused her face now and he took pity on her. 'Will you sit, ma'am?'

She nodded, adding: 'But let's go into the parlour.'

'Surely.' The word 'parlour' reminded him of home: overstuffed furniture, an explosion of pictures, vases, knick-knacks — the image of a lost certainty. But the Thorntons' parlour was a huge room only lightly furnished, nothing fussy, everything fit for purpose and little more. She sat by the stone fireplace, he opposite: both chairs had backs and arms but only the sitting part was cushioned.

'Call me Amanda,' she said.

'A pleasure, Amanda.'

'I'm still sorry I was so quick to shoot, Jack.'

'No, you were right. I'd a gun in my hand.'

'But it's just not that kind of place around here anymore,' Amanda said, which wasn't exactly true, Ryder knew, but he realized what she meant, what she really meant. It just hadn't been a very ladylike thing to do. Except it had, in his book.

'It happened in the war, didn't it?' she said suddenly, changing the subject.

He nodded. 'We were attacking hastily emplaced infantry on the flank, intending to roll them up. It was supposed to be an easy job but the Rebs had brought up a small battery of horse artillery and hidden it in some trees. They hit us with caseshot as we approached. My horse was shot from under me, and on to me. You know the rest.'

'So you lost the battle,' she said.

'No, they were too close. Our second wave took them, but I wasn't caring much at the time.'

'There was no war out west, not to speak of.'

Ryder shrugged. 'It's done with. I try to forget it all now. That's one of the reasons that brought me out west.'

She smiled. 'I'm glad you're here, Jack. I promise not to shoot at you again.' And suddenly she changed tack again: 'Tell me about your home.'

'It was nothing special, just a house in Ohio. My parents died while I was away. The only inheritance to speak of was the house. I sold it to pay my way through law school.'

'So you really wanted to become a lawyer?'

'It seemed to be the only job I could

do. At the time there was a fair chance I'd always be on crutches.'

'And now?'

'I only know two things, the law of torts and leading a cavalry troop. I think my choice is made for me.'

'And you'll stay here?'

'If everything works out. I hope it does.'

'So do I,' she said, standing up. He stood up too. 'No, you sit. I'm just going to light the lamps.'

He obeyed. It was growing dark. He just hadn't noticed. But now he watched her lighting the lamps one after another, reaching up to them, the light on her face, a picture of grace and purity straight out of an oil painting.

Oh yes, he thought, he was staying here. This was indeed the place to make a new beginning.

Part Three

1

Dutton Mazer watched the main trail from town to the Thornton Ranch from a hummock a hundred and fifty yards from it, the top of which was scattered with bushes and clumps of tall grass making him invisible to the pair in the buggy on whom his Sharps rifle was trained.

There were two of them in the buggy, that damned Ryder and his fat lawyer partner, Bridger. He would have preferred to get Ryder on his own — he had nothing against Bridger, though he had nothing for him either — but he'd been waiting here for three hours already and he wasn't about to indulge in a fourth. This was Thornton land, after all.

So what about Bridger? His first inclination was to leave him untouched, unless of course he missed and hit him.

Shooting at a moving vehicle was difficult but he reckoned he could get in three shots before they would be out of practical range, and if he wasted all three they deserved to escape. But he knew from experience that he wouldn't. He could hit a standing man at twice that range and once had — some drifter he'd found in the northern section. He'd buried him and heard no more about it. The man just shouldn't have been on Mazer land.

And now Dutton Mazer almost shuddered recalling his delight in reaching out and snuffing out a life. He had felt like a god. Bridger would die too, he decided. It was even to the good that he was with Ryder. It would confuse matters. Everybody knew about the business with his hand but what had that to do with Bridger? He drew a bead and fired.

Bridger slumped down, obviously hurt. Damn! He'd been aiming for Ryder. The rifle needed adjustment. But there was no time for that now. He reloaded and aimed again. And was delighted anew by what he saw. Ryder had stopped the buggy and was examining his companion. Maybe he hadn't heard the shot?

He aimed for the head, a pity he couldn't see the face well enough to make out the expression. It would be good to see that as the bullet struck, shattering teeth and bone and smashing out the back of the skull in a mass of blood and brain.

He held back for a moment as he recalled the rifle was firing high. He lowered it, going for a body shot with the chance of a head shot if he missed, then he fired.

Whether Ryder heard the shot or had just worked out what was happening, Mazer saw him turn and look at him, and then the bullet struck.

The rifle was still firing high. It took his head off.

Mazer sighed. He set the rifle down and looked to his hand, still bandaged, now more by way of an aid to memory than anything else. He stripped it off quickly, stuffed the bandages in his pocket. He also pocketed the used cartridge cases. On the way down the hummock he'd also make sure he left no clear footprints.

He stood up, felt the blood surging in his veins. He'd paid back an insult in blood and that felt good, and no less good was Bridger's death — at his whim! He smiled at that.

But sound carried. Best to get out of here, now.

As he turned to go down the slope he knew he'd have to tell his father about this and that worried him more than a little. Not that Bull Mazer was averse to spilling a little blood now and then but he'd demand more reason for it than what he'd call petty revenge.

But Dutton Mazer had thought his way out of that rather well. It was commonly known that since he'd had some kind of accident on the Thornton spread Ryder had been seeing quite a bit of Amanda Thornton, driving out here in a buggy whenever he got the chance. That was mostly how he'd recognized him. As for Amanda Thornton, he couldn't stand her — insipid little bitch! — but whoever married her eventually got the Thornton spread and the south side of the river. Bull Mazer wouldn't want a newcomer getting that, and a lawyer to boot.

Reaching his horse Dutton Mazer laughed. As far as he could see, Ryder and Amanda had been made for each other, but not now of course. Yes, that was exactly the way to put it to Bull Mazer. Land. With him, everything was land, Mazer land.

Dutton's hand was still a little sore as he grasped the reins but so what? That would pass. It was a pity though that Ryder hadn't known the why or the who of it. But maybe in that last second, in that glance of his towards the hummock, he had?

Dutton Mazer profoundly hoped so.

2

Ryder was writing a will for Norman Tillith, the owner of the Duke's Delight saloon, and finding it a dull job, so much so that he felt an unlawyerlike desire to write down the truth — 'all rights in the said brothel ... the aforesaid pimp Norman Tillith — ' but he restrained himself. Nobody had appointed him censor of morals; in fact, his legal status was really that of clerk until he had been recognized by the court, presuming Judge Shaw did just that when he arrived tomorrow. Come to think of it, the original censors, the Roman type, hadn't bothered with mere words but men. They'd decided the weight of a man's vote and to gain the privilege they had first to work their way up to consul and command armies. All he'd managed was the command of a troop of horse.

He raised his pen. They'd been good lads, all of them. They were almost all dead now. He'd been lucky, though he had never felt that before. In all truth, he'd half regretted surviving. He'd studied for the law because that was all a cripple could do. It had been pride rather than desire that kept him working and even breathing. His men hadn't given in and he wasn't about to give in either.

He'd been due to go out to the ranch today but Bridger had changed things at the last minute without saying why. He'd been disappointed but he'd said nothing. The weekend was near enough and anyway he didn't need Bridger with him.

He sighed, dipped his pen in the ink and started again:

' . . . and I declare that the aforesaid properties and monies shall become the property and monies of my sister, Adele Beata Smith, of 136 Madison Road, Cato City, Indiana, her heirs and assigns — '

He stopped. Something was happening in the street, a commotion of sorts. Hell there was no hurry. Tillith had looked fit enough, there was no haste needed. He set down the pen and got to his feet.

As he went out onto the sidewalk he felt the merest twinge in his leg, remembered how it had been, and ignored it. The people were gathering around the livery stable and the previous noise had ceased, replaced by an ominous silence. He walked over. They were just standing and looking. After a moment he eased his way through and entered, and saw the buggy.

He was quite dead. Ryder had seen plenty of corpses and wasn't shocked by another. Sheriff Mason had gone easy. The bullet had caught him in the jaw, making a mess of his lower face, and out the back of his head. A rifle bullet — a pistol bullet hadn't that kind of power. He'd become dead between one breath and the next. But the buggy was Bridger's.

'What happened to Bridger?' he asked Wilson.

'At the doc's,' Wilson said, a little shakily. 'The horse brought the buggy home on its own. Bridger's been shot in the belly.'

So both of them had been shot. He looked to Tom Gill. 'Who did it, Tom?'

Tom Gill just shook his head. 'I rode with him for twenty years. He wasn't an easy man, Zack Mason, but you could ride through ten counties and not find a better.' He spoke slowly, in a kind of shock. Ryder had witnessed that before too.

'So you're going to leave him like that?' he snapped. 'Go and get the undertaker. He's probably outside with the rest. Tell him to save the bullet if he finds it.' Ryder guessed he wouldn't. 'Go on, get moving.'

Tom Gill shook his head but not in negation; he did as he was told, grateful that somebody was telling him what to do.

'You, Wilson, get the horse back in its

stall. You can clean up the buggy when you can. Get moving, man.'

'Yes, sir.'

Ryder suddenly recalled he was no longer the commander of a troop of horse. Strictly, this was none of his business. Except for Bridger, his employer, who'd been gut shot, poor devil. Maybe the sheriff had been the luckier.

Ryder turned on his heel and walked out through the crowd with such assurance it parted for him without a word as he headed for Bluett's office.

3

There was no one outside Doc Bluett's office. Ryder knocked and entered without waiting for an invitation. Bridger wasn't strictly his partner but he was close to it.

The outer office was empty and the curtain between it and the inner office had been pulled to. Ryder walked up to it, called out:

'Jack Ryder here.'

'Come in,' Bluett said, sounding harassed.

Ryder did so and immediately saw Bridger stretched out on Bluett's crude wooden operating table. Bridger's clothes had been partially stripped off, revealing his gross belly, patches of white still remaining amidst the blood. It was a wound the like of which he'd never seen — Bridger's paunch had been pierced from one side to the other. At first though it didn't seem very serious, he'd only been shot through his fat, but he was obviously unconscious and had been for a long while. The horse, not him, had brought the buggy back.

'How is he?'

'Not good,' Bluett said, gesturing with gory hands. 'Look, the wound itself isn't that bad. I'm cleaning it out, making sure no bits of cloth and the like are left inside to fester. When I've done that I'll pour half a bottle of whiskey into it, bind it up and it should heal. But he's in shock. The bullet hit him like an express train. Thank God it went straight through, but he's not a young man.'

It had been a heavy bullet, probably from a Sharps rifle. The combination of a heavy charge in the gun and the heavy bullet meant it packed a terrible punch.

'The abdominal cavity hasn't been penetrated?' he asked.

'No.' Bluett hesitated, then: 'You know something about medicine?'

'Just about wounds. I've seen enough,

on the battlefield and after.'

'Of course.' He hesitated again. 'What do you suggest?'

'Just what you said. But we need him conscious — once you've finished the surgery.'

Bluett nodded and then set to work, his scalpel moving swiftly. Ryder stepped back: Bluett wasn't too bad a surgeon. He was quick at least and that was the essential thing. With these new fangled anaesthetics that might change but Bluett wasn't exactly a new graduate.

'Done,' Bluett said and reached for the whiskey bottle.

'You don't have any pure grain alcohol?'

Bluett shook his head and a moment later poured raw whiskey into the still open wound. Bridger didn't stir. Ryder had been hoping he would.

'Save a little to pour over the stitches,' Ryder said.

'OK,' Bluett agreed, not in the least upset but rather relieved to have someone to share the responsibility with. 'We've been friends a long time,' he said as he stitched, as neatly as a seamstress and no less quickly.

'Yeah.'

And then it was done. The somewhat reduced paunch was redoused and again Bridger gave no sign as the raw alcohol touched the still raw flesh.

'It's deep shock,' Bluett said.

There was no doubt of that, and the chances were Bridger wasn't going to come out of it. He'd seen it before. Some men, for all they were not fatally or even badly wounded, just faded away. There was only one thing he knew to do. He looked to Bluett.

'Try anything,' the doctor said, as if reading his mind.

Ryder leaned over the body, took hold of Bridger's head but didn't move it. Then, in his parade ground voice:

'Bridger, can you hear me?'

Nothing.

Ryder slapped his face. 'Bridger, you fat lazy no good bastard, wake up! Otherwise you're going to die. It's easy to die, to just let it happen, but you're not going to do that, do you understand me?' He slapped him again, not hard, and threw in some more barrack room language, culminating in: 'He's laughing at you, the man who shot you. Can't you hear him laugh? The fat bastard's dying, hasn't the guts to live. He's not even badly hurt but he's so fat and lazy he won't make the effort!'

A blink?

'Bridger, it's me, Ryder. Bluett's here too. Wake yourself up!'

Bridger groaned.

Bluett took over, finding another bottle of whiskey. This time he poured some of it into his mouth and, after choking a little, Bridger awoke.

'Stop shouting at me, Bluett,' he said.

'I wasn't,' Bluett said. 'Have some more whiskey.'

Bridger didn't choke this time.

Bluett looked to Ryder, nodded. 'You did well, but then you've done it before.'

'Yes,' Ryder said, not adding that this was the first time it had worked.

'Who're you talking to?' Bridger said, turning his head a little. 'Ryder, was that you shouting at me?' Suddenly he looked back to Bluett. 'Hey, Doc, how am I?'

'You've lost half your paunch but you'll live.'

'Nothing else?'

'No.'

Ryder walked back beside the table and looked down. Bridger met his eyes. 'Who did it?' Ryder asked.

'I don't know. I was in the buggy, and the next thing I know, some young devil is shouting insults at me.'

'Bear a grudge if you like, but you're here to do it.'

'Yeah, I reckon so.' His eyes shut and he started to make odd grunting noises. Taken momentarily aback, Ryder looked to Bluett, saw he was smiling.

'The fat bastard's just asleep,' he said. 'He's snoring.'

Ryder saw there were tears of relief in his eyes.

★　★　★

Mayor Jackman met him as he emerged from the surgery.

'How is he?'

'He'll live,' Ryder said.

'Thank God!'

'And Bluett.'

'Indeed. But did he say — '

'No.'

'Ah, that's unfortunate. Have you any ideas?'

'I'd guess that Bridger wasn't the target, that the sheriff was. You'd know better than me the men who'd want him dead in these parts. What does Gill say?'

'That they'd ridden together for twenty years. I couldn't get much more than that out of him. He's in a bit of a daze.'

'It's his job all the same,' Ryder said. He didn't add that it wasn't the mayor's, whose magisterial writ ran no further than the city boundary and didn't take in felony murder either.

'It's a bad business, Mayor Jackman,' he said and walked back towards the law office. He still had a will to complete.

4

Bull Mazer wasn't ill named. He was maybe an inch over six feet with massive shoulders and arms. He wore a Colt like everyone else but on him it looked superfluous and almost was. His way of disciplining people was by use of his fists and Dutton Mazer was afraid of them, though being the apple of his father's eye he'd scarcely ever felt their force. Yet he still feared that one day Bull would pound him down like everyone else. Maybe this was the day.

'Let's ride, kid,' Bull said.

They mounted up outside the corral and rode north for a while, then Bull brought his horse to a stop. 'Here'll do, kid. Let's stretch our legs.' Bull didn't even tie up his horse, he just let the reins hang as if he knew no horse would ever run from him. And they never did. Dutton had perforce to do likewise.

'You've heard about the sheriff?'

'Sure, Pa.' He didn't add that he'd felt sick when he did. He'd had it on the best authority that it was Ryder who was going with Bridger to the Thornton ranch that day. He and Sheriff Mason were much of a size, with the same taste in blue suits. It could have happened to anyone.

'It's bad news when you kill a peace officer,' Bull went on. 'They feel the need to hang somebody, especially when it's a full county sheriff, duly elected and all.'

'I heard they'd no idea who'd done it.'

Bull snorted. 'Hell, kid, I can guess. I checked your Sharps rifle. It'd been fired recently. You'd been missing all day and the night before you'd been in town, sniffing around. I guess you were after the lawyer fella, Ryder.'

Dutton said nothing. He never lied to his father. He'd almost admitted it to him when he got back but put it off a day. Then he'd heard he'd really got the

87

sheriff and decided to say nothing. Which was no longer an option now. But he just didn't have any words.

'I'll take that as a 'yes',' Bull Mazer said.

'He'd been nosing round the Thornton girl,' Dutton said by way of justification.

'I know.' He stared at his son. 'I did some rough things to get this range, Dutt, and I'm not proud of 'em but I'd do 'em again. In turn, you'll maybe have to do the same.' Suddenly he reached out and caught him by the shirt. 'But while I'm alive you kill no man who isn't trying to kill you without asking me first! Got that?'

Dutton Mazer went cold. 'Yes, sir.'

'Good. Have you told any of the hands?'

'No.' That was true. He'd been afraid they'd have told his father.

'Good. Don't. There'll be a reward out. Some might suspect but so long as they don't *know*, none of 'em can betray you.'

'It'll blow over, Pa.'

'Don't count on that. And don't count on 'em having no evidence against you either. There are more lies told in court than out, believe me. But they won't try that so easy. With you going and shooting the wrong fella, they might not even be so sure. All the world knows you'd nothing against the sheriff. and you'd have twenty alibis, including me.'

'So it's OK?'

'Maybe. A pity you didn't finish off the fat lawyer. I've problems with him.'

'Problems, Pa?'

'You recall McIver?'

He did, he and his father had been partner on the range fifteen years back. McIver had held title to the land just north of the river, but they'd shared, run their herds together. He'd been killed at round up and his land had come to the Mazers. 'Yes, Pa.'

'There's a little problem over title to his land. He left it to me in his will all right, but it turned out he hadn't registered the land properly.'

'But I've seen the county title map. It says — '

'What I paid for it to say. I haven't been able to change the dockets at the state capital yet.'

'But Pa, without the river — ' Dutton broke off.

'Yeah, we'd be doing well to take two hundred head to the railroad, and scratch cattle at that. But don't worry about that, kid. I'll see to everything.'

'Yes, Pa.'

'Ride on back now, keep your mouth shut and stay out of town till I tell you different. OK?'

'Yes, sir,' said Dutton, very much the dutiful son.

★   ★   ★

Bull Mazer watched the boy ride back, chastened a bit for now but that wouldn't last. The lad still had guts, but some of his mother's flightiness too. Pity he'd had to bring him up on his own but she'd run off with his foreman when the kid was five, along with the contents of the money chest. Not far or fast enough, though: he'd caught them in the mountains, killed 'em Indian style and hidden the bodies in a pile of talus.

Yeah, he owed the boy something. Like clear title to the land, and all this business made that very difficult. Dead sheriffs queered the pitch a great deal. But Dutton would have this range, no doubt of that. He'd keep the river land whatever it took. A pity the boy and that Thornton girl didn't get on. He'd had hopes. That would put the Mazer brand on the whole region.

An idea surged up from below. Maybe it was possible still. It could mean something like range war though, and hard deeds indeed. It was an option, but only in extremis. But one thing was sure: they'd not hang his kid, or take the Mazer name off this land.

There was nothing at all he wouldn't do to stop that.

5

Bridger watched the light fade in the window of the upper storey room. He was still woozy and his stomach felt as if he'd been kicked by two mules in succession but he didn't doubt that he would live.

Or that if it hadn't been for Jack Ryder, he'd be dead. Bluett had said so and while he wasn't the best doctor in the world, he was no liar. And no fool either. Besides, he could remember Ryder shouting at him, rather like a drill sergeant calling him back to duty.

Was life a duty? It was a potentially deep thought and he set it aside. He suddenly found he didn't care to think about big things, profound things. Or even about who had shot him. It was done, not to be undone. Just survived.

He watched the room turn dark. It was something he hadn't done since he was a kid, not light a lamp or a candle but just watch reality turn half unreal, watch the shadow grow and connect until there was scarcely anything but shadow.

The shadow had almost encompassed him, he suddenly realized. One day it would, but that was a profound thought too.

He found his mind wandering back to when he had first come out west, a duff lawyer from a pretty ropey law school. It had still been a federal territory then and, except when the Army got involved, everything had been pretty loose. It wasn't all that tight now, he thought, and would have laughed if his stomach didn't feel more stitched than a fresh made quilt.

He remembered the Indians. Never many — they weren't on the annual path of the buffalo — and it was much too open country for the Apache or the Navajo to fight over. Too poor too: it was good for raising cattle and nothing much else, and you needed a hell of a lot of it even for a single head.

At the beginning, he'd considered moving on, to San Francisco say, but there would have been lawyers aplenty there already, from more respectable law schools and he'd known he'd probably have ended up clerking in a store. So he'd decided to stay, to become a medium sized fish in a small pond.

Was I right? he asked himself and realized such questions just didn't have answers. Not only could no one predict the future, you couldn't predict a 'future' in the past either. Anything could have happened. He could have arrived in 'Frisco, got drunk and drowned in the bay, or taken a wrong turning, arrived too far south only to trip over a boulder sized gold nugget. He laughed but only briefly: it really did hurt too much.

The odd thing was, he'd been satisfied with a backwater and it wasn't quite that any longer. The railroad had seen to that. Tamar City was never going to rival New York but while there were stockyards in Chicago and people with an appetite for beef, it would be a place of some importance. Hell, if things worked out, he might indeed end up a judge

Why not? Even if he'd started out as a mediocre lawyer, he was a damned good one now. Experience helped and he'd read all his law books from cover to cover several times over. Shoot, there hadn't been much else to do most of the time. He'd heard of some cowpokes of a like mind who ended up compulsively reading the labels on cans!

Damn it, he was tired. Where was Bluett? He was supposed to be looking after him. But he really didn't need to ask. Bluett had gone for a drink. Bluett was a doctor like he'd been a lawman to start with, but he'd never developed any ambition at all. He didn't re-read his medical books for sure and —

The wooziness was growing. Had he been given something? Chloral hydrate, say? No, he'd have been out by now. It was just weariness. That worried him for a moment. Could it be . . . Hell, if he was going to wonder every time he went to sleep whether he'd wake up again, he really would drive himself into an early grave. It was just ordinary tiredness. He'd had, come to think of it, one hell of a day.

Part Four

1

Ryder awoke to the knocking on his hotel room door. He hesitated a moment before answering, recalling the events of yesterday, but he had no gun and besides, assassins don't knock. It turned out to be Deputy Gill.

'They want to see you,' he said.

'Who?'

'Mayor Jackman, Mr Bridger — '

'He's at the surgery.'

'No, he's home now.'

'Who else?'

'You'll see,' Gill said. 'It's important.'

Ryder could get nothing more out of him so he splashed water on his face, dressed and accompanied him to the law office. The door was unlocked and they climbed the stairs to the small apartment where Bridger lived.

There were three there — Jackman, seated; Bridger on a couch with blankets over his legs and stomach, quite hearty for a man who had been close to death the day before; and Judge Shaw.

'Hello, Jack,' Shaw said from where he stood in the window. He was a tall man with dark piercing eyes and sleeked down grey hair.

'I didn't know you were here, sir. I thought you were coming this afternoon.'

'I was but Mayor Jackman here got on the telegraph to me yesterday. I had the train schedule moved up a bit.'

Ryder was impressed. Judge Shaw really had clout. But then he always had. He'd been a county attorney back in Ohio and a family friend before coming out west. It was he, having heard Ryder had finally got his law diploma, who had arranged everything.

'It's serious, Jack,' Shaw went on. 'There's a damn good chance we could have a ranch war on our hands. The railroad company wouldn't appreciate that, hence the favour.'

'You're not here by accident, lad,' Bridger said, his voice quite natural. 'Big things are happening, but not quite as expected.'

Thornton too had said something of the sort, Ryder recalled.

'I'll tell it, Stoney,' Shaw said. 'Hell, you should be in hospital.'

'People die there,' Bridger complained, but said no more.

'It started,' Shaw said, 'a way back with Bull Mazer.'

★ ★ ★

Ryder listened to the litany of crimes ascribed to Bull Mazer with cold amazement. He'd started, so far as they knew, as a comanchero with a sideline in scalp-hunting, this last in Mexico where it had been still legal. Then he had come north, after things had got too hot for him, laying hands on a piece of land north of the river but with no river frontage. He'd made a deal with a man called McIver to run their herds

101

together and they had. And then McIver died 'accidentally' but almost certainly murdered by Mazer. Both McIver's will and partnership agreement gave his land to Mazer but there was a slight problem. Mazer still didn't have clear title, McIver hadn't registered it properly or, if he had, the records were lost. But nobody had queried it then, especially as it left Mazer the biggest rancher hereabouts.

Odd things had happened, like the land office burning down 'by accident'. Still, it seemed Mazer didn't have complete access to the state records although the main state map showed his ownership, he paid taxes on the land after all, even if the supporting docket was empty.

'We've been waiting for him to get it filled,' Shaw said. 'With a forgery. We reckon we know he's bought an employee there. That would have been proof enough. But it won't happen now, I reckon. Killing a county sheriff frightens people off.'

'And you can prove none of this?' Ryder asked.

Shaw shrugged.

'We know more,' Bridger put in from his makeshift bed. 'Quite a few men rode onto Mazer land and didn't ride off it. His wife's supposed to have run off and left him years back but he probably killed her too.'

' 'Probably' scarcely makes a good case,' Ryder said. 'Unless we can prove he killed the sheriff and gunned down Stoney here, and we can't, we just don't have him. Indeed, the title dispute would work in his favour. A man with bad title's a fool to shoot the sheriff and stir things up. Besides which, as he's paid taxes on the land for many years it's virtually his now.' He looked to both Bridges and Shaw. 'You both know that.'

'But he doesn't,' Bridger put in. 'He's fought shy of lawyers for years. He doesn't know he's worrying about nothing.'

'Maybe,' Shaw said, 'but Jack's made

a good point. Bull Mazer's a bad 'un, but he'd nothing to gain. But if not him, who?'

Ryder hesitated, then: 'I think that neither Mr Bridger nor the sheriff were the intended victim, that the bullet was intended for me. I was going to the Thornton ranch until the last minute when Stoney told me otherwise.' He paused. 'I take it Sheriff Mason and Mr Thornton knew all you've just told me?'

'Yes,' Shaw said, confirming what in effect was a conspiracy, albeit a legal one.

'We wanted to bring him up to date,' Bridger put it, 'your courting came second.'

'But Dutton Mazer might well have thought it was me anyway.'

'But why should he want to kill you?' Shaw asked, puzzled.

Ryder told him, with additions from Bridger who, wounded or not, was enjoying himself. Ryder guessed he'd had at least half a bottle of whiskey.

'Then he's got away with it,' Mayor

Jackman said finally. 'Proving Dutton Mazer killed the wrong man is nigh impossible.'

Legally he was pretty much correct, Ryder knew, but he was a fool to argue law in front of three lawyers and he was missing the main point anyway. Bull Mazer wasn't a lawyer. He was a cornered rat with very sharp teeth indeed and now so far as he knew his son was being measured for a noose. He'd jump and slash.

Judge Shaw was quite the opposite of a fool and he showed it. 'You can always make a case, Mr Mayor, and Dutton Mazer is perhaps an easier target than his father.'

'But — '

Shaw silenced him. 'It's not up to us to make cases anyway. It's for the sheriff initially. And as of now there's no sheriff in this county. We need one. There's an obvious candidate too.'

'No,' Ryder said.

'It won't affect your status as a lawyer,' Shaw said. 'I'll recognize you as fit to practise at the state bar later this morning and then I'll appoint you to serve out Mason's term. I've a wire from the Governor concurring.' He paused briefly. 'It's a big job, and in the circumstances a man who fills it successfully will go a long way. You can't refuse.'

And Ryder knew he had no real choice. The implicit threat that he'd lose Shaw's favour wasn't to be disregarded. And without that he'd be done with here, and he had reasons for staying, one very much in particular. But no less than all that, he'd started this, by chance, quite unwittingly, but started it nonetheless.

'Then I won't, sir,' he said.

2

Ryder walked slowly but easily back from the railroad depot towards the sheriff's office after seeing off the circuit judge. Thanks to Shaw he was now both a member of the state bar and the sworn county sheriff, a man of substance and power. A county sheriff was more than just a peace officer, he was the chief county executive, a collector of taxes, in effect the county governor — a man with a political future in the state if he wanted it. Shaw had done very well by him and might still do more, for he was very much the coming man. The train had been virtually a private one, coming and going at his wish, and that showed more clout with the railroad than that of an ordinary circuit judge.

Ryder entered the sheriff's office and saw Tom Gill seated at his small table to the right. How would he feel about being passed over?

'The badge is on your desk, Sheriff. The keys are in the drawer.'

'Thanks, Tom.'

'I'll stay on here while you still don't have your own man,' Gill added lugubriously.

'You can make that permanent, if you like.'

Gill brightened a little. 'For a while then, but it won't be permanent. It don't make sense now.'

Ryder picked up the simple, silver badge, looked at it a moment then pulled back his jacket and pinned it on his vest. 'Why not?'

'Didn't they tell you? Horace Mason left me his ranch. I worked for and with him for twenty years so he left it to me free and clear.' Tom Gill shook his head dolefully.

'Then you scarcely need a deputy's job.'

Gill looked at him. 'I'll still stay on a while, if I can. Thing is there's too many memories here.'

Ryder suppressed a smile. It was strange to think of Gill as a sentimental man. 'Stay as long as you want, Tom. I need all the help I can get. Judge Shaw's just left and I'm pretty much on my own.'

'If you need help for an arrest, he can arrange it. He's close with the railroad. He provided four railroad detectives to help out with the hanging last year.'

'If he can arrange that, he must be.'

'You know the railroad, they're close to anyone who might be useful to 'em. Talk was, they wanted to extend the spur line but nothing came of it.' Gill shrugged the matter aside, then: 'Truth is, I reckon I'm going to sell the ranch. Maybe after round up.' He looked up. 'You wouldn't be wanting to buy it now, would you, sheriff?'

Ryder shook his head. 'No, but I'll let you know if I hear of anybody who does.'

* * *

Being sheriff, Ryder decided, was more akin to being a cavalryman than to being a lawyer so he went back to the first thing he'd been taught — reconnaissance. He needed the lie of the land and knowledge of both the opposing and allied forces. The Mazers were easy. The office map along with town gossip gave all the information he needed. They were *there*, they had so many men. Not in itself very useful as he wasn't about to go out in battle against them. Suspicion was one thing, proof another. And there was none to be had in town. These last three days he'd visited every establishment, shown the town its new sheriff and listened to its complaints, always steering the conversation to Mason's murder.

If he were a good judge of men nobody in town doubted that Dutton Mazer's Sharps had done the deed but nobody would say it right out. Dutton's Colt six-shooter was just as swift and deadly, and behind him was his father, Bull Mazer, the fear of whom approached awe.

Ryder didn't share it. A writ or a subpoena brought any man down to size, however large his acreage.

He caught sight of the map spread over the office desk, yellow in the lamplight, and suddenly the map told him everything. It told him exactly why Shaw and his cabal were so interested in the Mazer spread too.

It wasn't really about the stolen McIver acres. It was about the spur line. It cut into the map on a south easterly diagonal and then stopped short before it touched Mazer land. But railroad companies wanted lines that didn't just hang in the air; they liked lines that connected with other lines, brought in other cities, and the merest glance at the map showed the only possible route to the nearest town, Placer Hills, ran through the Mazer spread. Not the good lands either but the dry part in the west.

That made sense of everything. Usually, a railroad could simply take the land under the law of eminent domain, but this was just a spur line. They'd have to buy it fairly. But suppose Mazer had refused . . . Heck, there was no supposing about it. He had. He couldn't sell. You don't let other men's surveyors even near land with a dubious title. The railroad was stymied. But if it were possible to break that title anyway, let the land revert to the state, then well connected people could buy it for a song and sell the right of way to the railroad at no small profit to themselves. A consortium say, headed by Judge Shaw. He'd get much more than money out of it. Railroad influence was powerful in this and all states. State attorney general? Governor? Both, probably, in that order.

Ryder wasn't shocked. So Bull Mazer was being shafted. Somebody usually was, and for once it couldn't happen to a more deserving fellow. Maybe it wasn't the kind of ethics they taught in law school but that was school, this was real life. And nobody had asked him to get his hands dirty. Judges dealt with ownership of land, not sheriffs. Maybe he ought to insist on every jot and tittle of the law but then what about his casual admittance to the state bar? In fact, it could finish him here; he'd lose Amanda. And even the thought of that was painful.

He folded up the map, put it in the drawer and went out onto Main Street. Somewhere out there Deputy Gill was making the evening rounds. All the lamps were lit for all it wasn't full dark and, almost despite himself, he felt a sudden liking and warmth for the ramshackle little city that was also the county seat. He'd been very lucky indeed since he came here.

But he'd obligations too: he'd sworn an oath to keep its peace and he wasn't keeping it too well when Sheriff Mason's murderer walked free. It was impossible for a city and it's county to have its sheriff murdered and nothing be done to avenge him. The law had to find a way.

And then he knew. There was a charge he could bring against Dutton Mazer. He had two viable witnesses and it was serious, serious enough to arrest him for it and hold him, and in the end, perhaps, lead to his hanging for murder. If it involved a little stretching of the truth, it still didn't quite break it.

He glanced across at the wooden court house, the local fount of justice. A nice word and when Tamar City had a neo-classical city hall and court house, someone would surely carve it over the entrance. In Latin, no doubt, and maybe there would be perfect justice here then. In the meantime, the rough and ready sort would have to serve.

3

Amanda Thornton was not best pleased. Ever since the Mason shooting she'd been confined to the ranch, effectively to the ranch house itself. Jack hadn't visited once since it happened and now they'd made him sheriff it was unlikely he'd be doing much visiting for a while from sheer lack of time.

And that annoyed her intensely. She'd liked him instinctively and the frequency of his visits suggested that she was reciprocated, but suddenly everything was different. She hadn't gone to town much before because the ranch had been her whole world. And besides, Tamar City was nothing to boast about, a railroad with one schoolhouse, one church, a general store, a feed store, a livery and more than a few saloons of the most

115

disreputable kind. Nothing for her.

And suddenly it was different. Now the ranch was a very small world indeed and Tamar City exciting because Jack was there.

She stared out of the window and watched her father drive off into town on the rig, Joe Bufuss next to him sporting a rifle, and she wished again he'd agreed to take her. But he hadn't and she could understand why. All the same, nobody was going to shoot her. Sheriff Mason had had enemies; he'd put people in jail, even hanged a couple a year back.

The thought came to her that if they found Mason's killer and convicted him, it would fall to Jack to hang him. She didn't like that idea at all. But would it make any difference to how she felt about Jack Ryder?

No. The answer came instantly. He'd been in the war, he'd killed people. At least, she guessed he had. Aside from just that one time, he would never talk about it, to her or to anyone, she guessed. So if he had another unpleasant duty now, so what?

She went back to the parlour and sat facing the unlit fire. It would be months yet before it would be lit and then it would roar up the back of the stone chimney like —

No, it was no use trying to avoid the subject that way. How did she feel about Jack Ryder? Did she love him?'

She found she just couldn't answer that question. In all the novels — especially the dime novels she had sent from back east — it was easy. The heroine just had to look and swoon. But she didn't feel like swooning. She just liked him and cared about him and missed him. She found she was hugging herself as if she were cold, almost wishing the fire was lit and burning away before her.

Part Five

1

Dutton Mazer knew good advice when he heard it and his father's to the effect that he should stay out of town was surely that, but like all advice it was easier to give than receive. A Saturday night at the ranch was worse than a Sunday morning in church. His father mightn't sing atrociously but he snored very loudly as he sat before the cold fireplace digesting a massive meal of beef.

The other alternative was the bunkhouse and the company of the few cowboys who could resist the temptations of the saloons and their upstairs rooms. There was always a game to be had, but only for nickels and dimes, and he invariably lost and then became the recipient of good advice once more. He was too rash. No one can beat the odds. A good pro will always beat a

121

good amateur. It was doubtless all true but it took the fun out of life.

As for the sheriff and the fat lawyer, they surely couldn't touch him now. Nobody'd seen him shoot anybody, and he hadn't anything against either of them to speak of. Hell, they probably didn't even know it was him. In fact, by staying out of town he just made himself look guilty.

But he waited for the month end, when all the local cowhands would be in town, and went in late, sneaking into 'The Black Queen' — not his usual haunt — by the back door, even leaving his horse tied up out back; his saddle was distinctive.

The gamblers were happy to have him at the table. Whiskey flowed and he won the first two hands — small but comforting. The next hand he folded before he'd put much in the pot and only in the fourth, when his cards really came good, did he start shelling out. If the man in the silver vest hadn't had phenomenal luck he'd have taken the pot instead of losing over a hundred dollars. But for once he knew his limit; besides, the saloon felt rather too open. He kept glancing sidelong at the swing doors, expecting the sheriff or his deputy. Neither came but it took the edge off things. A room above would be much more private and relaxing. He caught the redhead in the yellow velour dress eyeing him and eyed back. She came over. A moment's conversation and she went up the stairs, looking back brazenly as she went.

'I'll be back,' Dutton said, vacating his chair, though he had no intention of returning. Still, it sounded good. He started up the stairs, pausing at the top to glance again at the doors.

No one.

He smiled to himself. Good advice go hang! This was the life. He glanced along the unfamiliar doors of the corridor, looking for number six — and, reaching it, knocked on it. One should be gentlemanly about these things.

'Come in, Dutton.' The voice was seductive.

'Yes, ma'am,' he said softly to himself opening the door and stepping inside.

She was sitting on the bed, still in the velour dress and looking rather apprehensive. Her glance flickered to the right. He followed it and saw Sheriff Ryder seated on a straight-backed chair aiming a sawn off at his belly.

'Close the door behind you,' Ryder said, 'and don't try anything funny. I wouldn't care to upset the lady by cutting you in half in her presence.'

Dutton did as he was bid.

'Now take off the gunbelt.'

Again, he did so. But by now he had regained his voice. 'Sheriff, what the hell is this? I'm not even drunk.'

'I'm glad to hear it,' Ryder said. 'It means you'll do nothing foolish. We're leaving by the front this time, not the back way you came in. You go first. I'll be behind you and this gun will be on you all the way. So don't call out for help. If I so much as suspect a gun's raised against me, guess what I'm going to do . . . '

Dutton didn't need to guess, and he didn't have to guess what two barrels of a sawn off at close range would do either.

'What the hell's this about?' he asked. An innocent man would ask that.

'Attempted murder. Other charges may follow.' Ryder stood up. 'Heck, I hardly knew the sheriff and Bridger's going to be okay so I've no personal animus in this, if you follow me. But I'll do my job, never doubt it. Now get moving'

Dutton didn't doubt it at all. He got moving.

2

'This is unbelievable,' Lawyer Tomkins said, examining the charge sheet. 'I was given to understand he was being charged with the attempted murder of Lawyer Bridger, with a view to adding the charge of murder of Sheriff Mason before trial.'

'We'll agree to that,' Bridger said. 'Just get your client to confess.'

'This is a privileged discussion,' Tomkins said. 'Anyway, it's common gossip.'

'That's true,' Ryder admitted. 'But we're all lawyers here and know that gossip's one thing, the law's another.'

'Indeed,' Tomkins said. 'And congratulations on your admission to our bar, Sheriff Ryder. Though it's rather odd to begin by becoming sheriff.'

'But quite legal and indeed admirable,' Bridger said. He sat heavily in his chair, a blanket wrapped round his shoulders. His wound was drained and was healing well but he was still an invalid. All the same he had insisted on coming to the sheriff's office for this meeting.

'No doubt, but this says Dutton Mazer attempted to kill a prostitute by drawing his gun and aiming it at her and was prevented from firing it by the sheriff here. But over a month ago. It's obviously just a holding charge, not to say a fixed up one.'

'Whatever her profession — and the charge sheet doesn't mention it — it's still a crime.'

'So why didn't you arrest him then?'

'Because I wasn't sheriff then,' Ryder said, 'and the young lady didn't lay a charge at the time.'

'The grand jury will throw it out.'

Bridger smiled. 'It's going direct to the circuit judge. As you know, in special circumstances he can dispense with a grand jury indictment and proceed straight to trial.'

Tomkins sighed. Shaw would obviously go along with it. He tried a different tack. 'What if he pleads guilty to a lesser charge, drunk and disorderly, say?'

'As acting county attorney I don't feel able to reduce the charge,' Bridger said. 'I know guns are often drawn but to draw and aim is still attempted murder and if it hadn't been for Ryder here, it might indeed have been murder.'

'So what sentence are you asking for?'

'Fifteen years.'

Tomkins literally threw up his hands. 'This is a railroading!'

'I resent that,' Bridger said. 'We have two witnesses. One is dubious, that I will allow, but Ryder here is a member of the state bar and the highest official of the county. Of course nobody can predict a verdict but supposing it were 'guilty' I can't see a sentence of less than ten years being imposed.'

'And there is no way you'd deal? None whatsoever?'

'No.'

'Then I can do no more good here. I'll have a word with my client, if I may, then I'll visit his father before going back to the state capital. Let me know when the trial date is set.'

'Of course,' Bridger said.

★ ★ ★

Dutton didn't take the business well, shouting obscenities and imprecations from his cell. Ryder and Bridger went to the latter's office to avoid the noise. Nobody would break Dutton Mazer out and even if they did, that would render him a fugitive and liable to shooting on sight.

'In a way, I don't blame Dutton for not taking it well,' Ryder said as they entered the law office.

Bridger sat down and touched his somewhat reduced stomach. 'I've no sympathy whatsoever. It's a fit up, a railroading, call it what you like, but it's legal. You wouldn't be lying.'

'Not much, at least.'

'Courts aren't places for the whole truth whatever the books say,' Bridger said. 'Anyway, it was your idea and I guess there's a good chance it'll end up with a confession to Mason's killing.'

Ryder nodded, then: 'How will Bull take it?'

'Badly. But what can he do? He has no political friends of any use. He could try to buy off the girl but that's not his style. So what can he do but bluster?'

'Nothing. At least, I sincerely hope not,' Ryder said, somewhat sorry for thinking of it in the first place. It left a bad taste in the mouth.

'Hell, boy,' Bridger said, reading his expression, 'the man's a murderer. And this'll do your career no end of good.'

Ryder didn't argue, Bridger was right — this was the way lawyers worked. All the same he couldn't help feeling that the war had been cleaner. You killed your enemies openly and cleanly as they tried to kill you, not by back door methods. But the war was over . . .

3

Ryder walked out into the street and saw the life of Tamar City going on about him, nothing very exciting, there was a rig pulled up outside the feed store and sacks were being loaded on it; a pair of oldsters sat outside the general store smoking corncob pipes and talking; a woman and a very young child walked past him. All utterly ordinary. Peaceful. And then the thought came to him — the war really was over, utterly past and gone, and with it the need for extraordinary measures. Maybe Dutton had killed the old sheriff and wounded Bridger, but then surely the thing to do was to prove it and hang him legal, not frame him on a trumped up charge?

He was considering this when the horseman turned into Main Street riding as if all the devils in hell were after him. He rode straight for the sheriff's office, dismounted and was about to enter when Ryder called out to him.

'Over here.'

The man turned, his face white. 'The ranch, sheriff, the ranch!'

Ryder walked over to him. 'What about it?' he recognized him now; he was one of Thornton's men, a sober man too, oldish for a cowboy.

'It's burning,' he said, 'all of it, burning!'

⋆ ⋆ ⋆

Ryder had seen the smoke on the horizon almost as soon as they'd ridden out of town. For the past hour they'd been riding towards it and his stomach was still hard with fear. It had been almost impossible to get any sense out of the old cowboy, least of all whether Amanda or her father were safe.

He glanced at the ad hoc posse accompanying him. There were fifteen of them: substantial citizens, a few youths, the swamper from one of the saloons, the undertaker. Almost every single one of them had a six-gun strapped on and most had long guns in their saddle sheaths, but that was out of habit. You don't fight fire with guns. Or oaths, he hadn't sworn any of them in or even invited them along. They'd just come and that was impressive. A neighbour was in trouble . . .

* * *

It was worse than he'd thought possible. The flames were all gone when they got there though smoke still rose from the blackened ruins. Not much remained: all the buildings had been wooden and all had burnt virtually to ground level.

And there wasn't anyone standing around, either. It was as if there'd been no one left alive to do so. Including Amanda . . .

He dismounted and walked towards

the house, his chest tight with fear. She hadn't dominated his thoughts, but she'd rarely been out of them for long. Nothing had been arranged, no offer made or accepted but he'd known she would be his wife. He was certain he would be accepted. Now he only wished the words had been spoken.

The house had been reduced to its ground plan, walls, roof, floors burnt away, only a little of their detritus smouldering away, littering the odd bits of furniture which, for some reason or other, had survived — the piano, the intact frame of an iron bedstead, a table, its legs collapsed but the memory of its once polished surface gleaming still. Ryder walked into the ruin, going from room to room, looking, ignoring the acrid stench. But there was nothing there, no bodies, no —

'Sheriff!'

Someone was shouting at him, one of the posse.

'The barn, sheriff, the barn!'

He walked out of the now schematic

house and saw his boots were beginning to smoulder. He kicked them out in the dust and went to face the man.

'They've found 'em. Oh, God, they've found 'em!'

Ryder nodded and followed him, not trusting himself to speak.

★   ★   ★

The barn had gone up like a blast furnace — it had only the one upper floor but that had been filled with hay which must have poured downwards in flames like Greek fire and consumed all beneath it — and there had been many, including the horses. It had been a pitiless attack.

There had been a fight. There were guns scattered amongst the bodies, mostly six-guns, but none of the chambers were damaged too badly as they would have been if all six rounds had exploded simultaneously if they'd just been left to burn loaded. They'd been fired until they were empty.

'That's Thornton,' one of the posse members said.

'And Old Jake, look at the ring — '

Ryder turned away. Let the locals sort out who was who. Amanda wasn't among them; there was enough skin and hair left, just, to see at a glance there wasn't a woman among them. That left the bunkhouse. He started for the door and then noticed the stalls to his left. Horses don't burn well. He'd seen battlefields and the aftermath of the same but this was something else again, something truly terrible. In a war you could understand the necessity of fighting to keep men in a building and then torching it, listening to their screams and still keeping up a hail of gunfire to confine them and doom them to horrible death. It was at least an act of war. But this was peace-time . . .

He met up with Jackman as he was going out.

'How bad is it?' the mayor asked.

'Bad. There's Thornton over there

and six men with him. I'm going to the bunkhouse — '

'I've just been there. It was empty when it burned.'

Which was what he'd hoped. He let out his breath. Amanda wasn't among the dead and never had she been intended to be. He relaxed a little and suddenly felt as if he were about to be sick. He must have gone grey for the mayor asked:

'You OK?'

'Maybe,' Ryder said. 'I'm sick to my stomach at what I've seen here but it could have been worse.'

The mayor looked at him.

'Amanda isn't among the dead.'

The mayor nodded as if understanding but he wasn't concerned with the girl, Ryder knew. He walked with him back to where the bodies lay and saw him go grey in turn.

'The — ' Jackman began and stopped in mid-curse for want of words bad enough. Then Ryder saw the undertaker standing by.

'Make me a list of the dead,' he said. 'Fetch the bodies into town. As ex-officio coroner I'll go along with your identifications. You can bury them when it suits you.'

'But Mr Thornton has a private plot here.'

Ryder shrugged, what did it matter where a man's bones lay for eternity? They were just bones. 'Bury him here then. But remember, let me have that list.'

'Yes, sir.'

Ryder turned and left. Oddly, he no longer felt in the least sick. The rules had changed suddenly. He'd been wrong to think the war was over. It had begun again, a smaller war but no less bitter, much more so in fact. He'd never hated his enemy then. He did now and all scruples, pity and morality could be set aside. He had one aim and he'd achieve it at any cost. He'd get Amanda back if he had to wade through blood to do it.

Part Six

1

'No,' Bridger said, examining the sheet of yellow paper.

'I say yes,' Ryder said.

Bridger shook his head definitively. 'I understand your feelings, Jack, but you can't let them override your duty. As county attorney, I just can't go along.'

Ryder smiled. 'As I recall you're county attorney because I appointed you. Sheriff Mason just appointed you case by case.'

'Still — '

'It seems to me, if I can appoint, I can dismiss too. But it won't come to that, I know. Read it again, carefully.'

Bridger did just that, slowly:

Let Dutton Mazer go free and you'll get Amanda Thornton back alive and well. Be quick.

'Well?' Ryder said.

'So what?' Bridger replied. 'Anybody could have written it. It's on paper off a yellow lawyer's pad and written in capitals, in pencil. Unidentifiable. For all I know you could have written it yourself.'

Ryder almost sighed. 'That's because you're thinking like a Philadelphia lawyer. We both know who wrote it and who had it pushed under the jailhouse door.'

'Knowing isn't proof.'

'It's proof enough. After the burning nobody in this town will doubt that's Bull Mazer's work. Maybe it would be part of a very thin case in court but then the chances of it ever getting to court are slight anyway.'

'Still — ' Bridger began again.

'I'm playing along, Stoney. All we really have Dutton on is a holding charge. Truth to tell, I'm sorry I ever trumped it up. The burning — '

'Wasn't your fault,' Bridger put in.

'I know that. I also know that once

free Amanda could testify. Bull Mazer would be facing multiple counts of murder and arson. You know what that means.'

'He'll never let her go.'

'I've still got to try. And haven't you noticed, this is getting to be a dangerous county for a man to travel around. I think Dutton needs an escort at least part of the way home.'

And suddenly Bridger understood, at least part of it. 'You'll get yourself killed.'

'Don't bet on it,' Ryder said.

Bridger smiled suddenly. 'I won't, lad, no indeed!'

2

For Dutton Mazer the day had started well. Ryder had wakened him just before dawn, told him he was being given bail. He'd looked glum about it too which obviously meant the charges would end up being dropped, and so he hadn't objected when instead of being allowed to go out into town he'd been taken out back where his horse was waiting for him, alongside Ryder's own.

'I'll see you out aways,' Ryder said.

Dutton's gun and gunbelt were hung around the saddle horn and when he looked to him, Ryder nodded. Dutton belted up, noticing there was no ammunition in the loops.

'The gun's empty too.'

Dutton had merely shrugged. It was a precaution he would have taken himself and there was plenty of ammo at the old homestead. He mounted up and followed Ryder out of town by various back ways, all going south which was odd but he reckoned the business had to be a humiliation to Ryder and he wasn't advertising it. He could understand that and he wasn't about to argue with the man, not with an empty gun and recalling the terrible force of his arms.

★ ★ ★

They'd ridden south for over ten miles and into some of the worst, scarcely grassed country hereabouts before Dutton began to worry.

'Hey, Ryder,' he called out.

'What?' Ryder asked, turning.

'Where the hell do you think you're going, Old Mexico?'

Ryder looked at him for a moment, then: 'No. Here'll do fine. Get down off your horse.'

'I thought I — '

'You heard me,' Ryder said, not making any motion towards his gun but there was no doubting he meant what he said. Dutton considered making a run for it but decided against it. Maybe Ryder intended a fight, *mano a mano*, and Dutton was up for that. He'd prefer to avoid it but strength alone wasn't everything. He knew some tricks that would make Ryder's eyes water. He got down from his horse. He started to unbuckle, preparatory to the fight.

'No, leave your gunbelt on.'

'Hell, I'm not drawing on you with an empty gun.'

'There'll be no fight,' Ryder said and dismounted himself. He collected both horses and led them to a long, scraggy sage bush and tied them to it. Then he took the lariat off Dutton's horse and approached him.

'Sit down.'

'What — '

Ryder tapped the butt of his six-gun. 'There's nobody to hear, Dutton. Do as you're told.'

It was true, they were in the middle of nowhere and chances were they could sit down here for a year and see no one. And there was something about Ryder's tone that brooked little argument. He sat down.

Ryder tied him up, much more expertly than he'd have expected from a lawyer. Ryder said nothing as he did it and when he had finished he just walked off, taking out a cigar and lighting it. Dutton tried to get himself in a comfortable position but only succeeded in falling over on his side. He couldn't get back up. 'Hey, Ryder!'

But Ryder just walked further away. Dutton tested his bonds again. Could he slip out of them? No, there was no chance. He began to worry. He wondered if his pa was about to collect him and Ryder was just making sure the odds weren't two to one. But Ryder wasn't looking out for anyone. He was just walking about smoking cheap cigars. Passing the time. Before what?

Time slowed to a crawl. He kept easing himself from one side to the other but the gravelly surface of the land dug into him and the tight bonds cut into him too. And it was getting hotter.

Noon. It wasn't full summer but the sun was still hot. He watched Ryder walk over to the horses and take one of the canteens. Dutton could almost taste the water Ryder was surely about to give him but Ryder merely took a couple of sips himself and closed the canteen up.

'Hey, give me a drink!'

Ryder walked over. He didn't bring the canteen. 'No,' he said, 'I'm going to watch you die of thirst.' And with that he turned about and walked off.

Dutton was too stunned for words. First he was being let go and now this. For what? For killing the sheriff? Hell, Ryder had hardly known him and Bridger had only been wounded. Besides, Ryder was a lawyer and not even lawyers liked each other that much; usually, hardly at all. He's bluffing, he thought, he wants me to sign a confession. Then I get the water.

And, later, hanged. The devil with him!

The sun seemed to stay high forever. He could feel the sweat on his skin and resented it as a waste of water. Keep calm, he told himself, it's only a bluff. But Ryder didn't look like a man who was bluffing. And, come to think of it, he hadn't asked for anything. Dutton called out:

'Sheriff.'

Ryder walked over, smoking his sixth cigar. He just looked at him.

'What do you want?' Dutton asked.

'Did I say I wanted anything?'

'A confession maybe?'

'That you murdered Mason? I know that. Confess or deny it, it doesn't matter. Hell, if you gave me a signed confession do you know what I'd do with it?'

'No.'

'I'd tear it up into little pieces and throw it away. It doesn't matter any more. I'm not trying to convict you, I'm just going to kill you.'

'Damn it, what have I done to you?'

Ryder looked at him a moment before answering, then: 'You tried to kill me for one thing. But as I wasn't there at the time I forgive you that. Of course, in the usual way of things I'd still convict and hang you for it but it's past that now.'

'You mean the Thornton ranch business? I'd nothing to do with that. Hell, you can testify to that. You had me in your jail. I wouldn't even have known about it if you hadn't let Shorty Travers in to talk to me last night.'

Ryder extracted his cigar and knocked off the ash. 'I never said you did.' He paused. 'Sheriff Mason was just business, but I was going to marry that girl. Now I won't. So I'm taking something in return away from Bull Mazer.'

'What? Dutton asked, stupefied.

'You.' And with that he turned and walked off, a moment later putting his cigar back in his mouth and re-igniting it by drawing on it.

Hell, he doesn't mean it! Dutton thought. But he found it harder than ever to believe that. There was something very convincing about Ryder. And he knew all the tales about men dying from thirst. How the tongue swelled up until it choked you, but not quite: you weren't so lucky. He'd heard of men tearing their fingernails out as they scrabbled at the earth for water. Except he wouldn't do that. He'd just have to lie here with that buzzard Ryder smiling down at his agonies.

But Ryder wouldn't smile even then. He never seemed to smile. He just looked on, coldly, calculatingly. He —

Keep calm. There was a way out. Even if he couldn't sensibly take it, there was a way out. He only had to tell —

But he couldn't do that. He'd be betraying everything, everyone.

And yet there was an awful dryness in his mouth. Was his tongue beginning to swell? He moved it around in his mouth. It felt different. There was less space between it and the roof of his mouth. Even as he thought about it, it seemed to swell appreciably.

Imagination. Yes, that was all it was. Keep calm.

He moved, trying to stop the ground cutting into him so hard. His back ached now and the bonds were twisting into him like drying rawhide. He looked across at Ryder, saw him watching him, smoking yet another of those damned cigars.

He's enjoying it. Hell, he could understand a man paying off debts, enjoying that even, shooting someone even, but to stand there and watch a man die of thirst was beyond his conception. Especially as Ryder was so cold about it, not a flicker of anything, just those cold blue eyes watching him, watching for —

He coughed. His tongue *was* swollen. He tried to spit but couldn't. Hell, it was damn near filling his mouth. And all the time Ryder was there, watching, waiting.

He had to —

No, Ryder would back down. He just

wouldn't go through with it. No man could watch another die of thirst.

Except maybe Ryder. He recalled the strength of the man that first night back at the hotel. It was as if he'd been caught in a vice. Utterly inhuman.

He looked up, saw the sun still scarcely past its zenith, felt the heat beating down on him and felt himself sweating out precious water, felt water running down his cheeks. But that wasn't sweat, it was tears. He was weeping out of sheer fright.

Ryder walked over to the horses, drank sparingly from one of the canteens, spat most of it out, looked at him and then lit another of those damned cigars. What kind of man was he? Just what the hell kind of man was he?

3

Dutton broke just two hours after noon, except he didn't just break, he dissolved. His tongue was choking him, he was dying and he was panicking. Which was what Ryder had intended all along. The Duttons of this world rarely had cold courage, courage that persisted when they were on their own and victory unlikely. With a band of followers, Dutton could be passably courageous. A touch of sun and a touch more of imagination had turned him into a jelly.

'She's not dead!' he burst out, forgetting his tongue was choking him.

'You're lying,' Ryder said coldly, daring him on.

'No, Bull was going to use her as a bargaining counter to free me. Shorty told me. She wasn't harmed.'

Ryder drew on his cigar, letting his

silence speak for him. His own mouth felt dry from the cigars, which had struck him — correctly — as a useful stage prop.

'I know where she is, where they're holding her.'

'So you say.'

'For God's sake, give me a drink!'

'If I really thought she were alive, maybe. But you'd say anything.'

'No, I'll tell you. I killed the sheriff. I shot Bridger.'

'Why?'

I was trying to kill you.'

'So I should give you a drink for that?' Ryder forced a smile. It worked. Dutton's already grey face went white.

'I'll sign anything!'

'I told you, I don't care. Bull's going to pay for the girl; she's disappeared, so will you.'

At the word 'disappeared' Dutton had a choking fit, obviously imagining himself being dumped in a shallow grave.

Ryder chose that moment to go and

have a drink, letting a little of the water spill as he did so.

'For God's sake, she's at the old sod house. When Bull first came here he only had land in the north. He built there. He only spent a year or so there and left but he never let it get too bad. It's a good place to store things . . . and people.'

'Who's with her?'

'Old Troon and young Terry Miller. Bull said he wanted to keep her in a saleable condition — Troon's too old to care and Miller's still wet behind the ears.'

He was obviously quoting Shorty Travers, the Mazer hand who'd been hanging around the jail for days and who had probably been the one who had 'posted' the ransom note. Certainly Dutton was too stressed to make up things like that, so he was necessarily telling the truth. Ryder took out his knife, walked over to him. Dutton's eyes grew very large.

'I believe you,' Ryder said, cutting the

cords from Dutton's wrists. Dutton virtually screamed as the circulation came back, his thirst temporarily forgotten.

'Just one thing,' Ryder added, 'I want what Shorty Travers said to you in writing.' He dug into his pocket, brought forth a blank sheet of quarto and a stub pencil.

Dutton, still rubbing his wrists in considerable pain, looked at him appealingly, almost dog-like.

'Hell,' Ryder said, 'just sign your name on the bottom. We'll fill it in later.'

Gratefully, Dutton did so. Ryder took back the pencil and paper and fetched him the canteen. He didn't advise him not to drink too much, too fast. This Dutton did and spent several minutes coughing and spluttering. When he had done, Ryder said:

'Lie on your back, feet in the air.'

Dutton did so without protest and Ryder cut his legs free. The pain of lost circulation there was even worse. Ryder took the time to wash the taste of the cigars out of his mouth.

'Now we're going to get Amanda Thornton back,' Ryder said. 'And you're going to help.'

'No.'

'Yes. Do you think getting shot's OK, better than dying of thirst? Believe me, you'd be just as dead'

But it was hardly needed. All the courage was leached out from Dutton. It would come back, by dribs and drabs, but for the moment he was safe enough.

'They'll kill her if they have to,' Dutton said. 'If they saw you and a posse — '

'There'll be no posse, just you and me.'

Dutton said nothing. Even the malevolence had left him. Ryder felt no pride in what he'd done but no shame either. Only necessity.

'Here, have another drink,' he said.

4

As they rode Ryder kept Dutton Mazer ahead of him. As he'd need him to appear to be free for the scheme to work he had taken the precaution of tying Dutton's feet together under the horse's belly. This wouldn't stop him riding off but while a man was a small target, a horse was a big one and unless he wanted to be crushed under his horse he'd not be trying any madcap escapes.

The route was a long curve east of town. They'd crossed the railroad track an hour back and they were making good time, they'd be at the sod house before sundown.

Dutton let his horse slow so he was almost level with Ryder.

'Move forward a little.'

'Hell, it's hard to talk when you're behind me.'

'All the same, you will.'

'OK, OK, no need to get tough about it. You still sore at me?'

Ryder noted that he was talking like a kid trying to wheedle his way back into an adult's good books. But he went along all the same. Maybe he'd learn something. 'Hell, why should I be? It's just business now. After all, you never actually took a shot at me and I didn't hold you responsible for the Thornton business.'

'Because I was in your jail at the time,' Dutton said winningly, that at least was the intention.

'Surely.'

'You know, I've been thinking about how to get the girl out of the house.' He turned briefly to look at Ryder, smiling, and the smile was 'winning' too.

'And?'

'I reckon if you let me go in on my own, no gun, at least no ammo for it, I can just tell them to let her go. They'll think I'm talking for my pa and there'll be no trouble.'

Except he'd instantly commandeer some ammunition and there'd be three of them shooting back at him. A child could see through that plan but for all that, Dutton wasn't stupid. In most ways he was even pretty bright.

No, Ryder thought, the problem was that Bull Mazer had done a truly terrible job raising him; he really was spoilt rotten. On the ranch he'd been the boss's son, denied nothing; in town, the future biggest landowner around, likewise to be coddled and pampered by everyone who could see a future profit in it. The result was that he just wasn't a proper adult — he was a big, vicious kid, so used to getting his own way, to seemingly being believed when he was obviously lying, that he was scarcely able to look after himself. Even that time in the hotel he'd been about to shoot either the drab or his pal simply because he'd been stymied.

'Maybe I can trust you,' Ryder said carefully, 'but could I trust those two?'

'They'll do what I tell 'em.'

Ryder said nothing.

'You really wouldn't have let me die of thirst back there, would you?'

'No,' Ryder said. He didn't add that it would have taken too long. The supposed rule of three — three minutes without air, three days without water and thirty days without food was the crudest rule of thumb. He could well have lasted six. If it hadn't worked . . . but it had.

'I like Amanda Thornton,' Dutton said suddenly. 'Trouble is, she don't like me.'

'That's the way of it,' Ryder said. 'Let's be getting a move on, we want to get there before nightfall. Otherwise they might not recognize you and shoot you by mistake.'

'Yeah,' Dutton said, 'that'd be a hell of a note.' He touched spurs.

Ryder followed, glad to have the conversation over. There was no pleasure in exchanging pleasantries with a man he might have to hang.

5

Amanda sat on the plank bed in the tiny bedroom of the sod house, arms about her knees, staring up at the tiny window. Two iron bars had been set in it cross fashion, making the room doubly a prison, though they were so rusty she guessed the original purpose had been to keep people — presumably Indians — out, not her in. But it scarcely mattered.

They were going to kill her, she knew, and she was afraid. She knew she ought to be angry too, for her father and the rest, and she was, but it was fear that was dominant. All the world must think her dead in the fire so now her captors could do what they wanted with her. It was as if she didn't really exist. Except perhaps to suffer.

But so far she'd been dealt with kindly enough here in this place. Her jailers were an oldish man and a boy and they were even polite. They'd been with her since they'd dragged her out of the house before setting fire to it. She'd seen everything. The barn was already blazing when they tied her to a horse and brought her here, to this awful, damp dirty place. But thereafter they'd been kind enough, even respectful.

How could they be both part of such a horror and then just human? Because they were just followers. When Bull Mazer said 'shoot her' she didn't doubt they'd do it, respectfully but quickly. And maybe that was the best she could hope for.

She'd been thinking about Jack Ryder a lot, but without hope. He was certain to think she was dead. Her father had liked him too and approved of their unspoken understanding though he'd said he thought him a little too civilized for these parts. She knew better. Indeed, that was the only fault she could see in him — a ruthless single-mindedness that was capable of anything. His leg had been agony for him — Doc Bluett was no respecter of his patients' privacy — and yet he'd never let himself be seen limping. That was a kind of strength she could barely conceive of, let alone approve of, for all she knew it would never be turned against her.

It would be turned against Bull Mazer but by then she would be dead. All the same, it was better to think of that than give way and weep. Everything had come right in her life, everything she'd ever wanted had been almost in her grasp . . . and then plucked away and here she was, hours or days away from a nameless grave and maybe worse in between. But she would not weep. Better to think of Bull being —

But it wouldn't work. She didn't care about him. She stared at the barred window and waited patiently for nothing without tears or wailing. Ryder would never know but if he did, he wouldn't be ashamed of her . . .

Suddenly strength wasn't enough and

she felt tears running down her cheeks, not for her father but tears of pity for herself. She rubbed them angrily away then sat as before, tightening her grip about her knees.

6

The sod house was built into the side of a small hillock. From a distance it looked almost picturesque; close up you hardly needed to imagine the poverty and misery involved in living there. The Great Plains were spotted with their like, Ryder knew. The west was only a land of milk and honey in the eastern imagination.

There were no horses in evidence; he guessed they were tethered behind the hillock somewhere.

'Careful,' he said to Dutton. 'I'm right behind you. If they shoot at me they'll probably hit you.'

Dutton laughed. 'No problems.'

Ryder disagreed in silence. It all struck him as a very dangerous way of proceeding but he still couldn't think of a better. A posse could have surrounded the place but once the bullets had started to fly Amanda would have been just as likely to be hit as her captors. This way she had a chance. The pair were used to obeying Dutton and it was in his interests to get her out alive.

A figure emerged, an oldish man in a plaid shirt. He was holding a full length Greener shotgun.

'Dutton,' he acknowledged.

'We've come for the girl, Troon.'

'With the sheriff there?'

'We've done a deal,' Dutton said with causal conviction.

'I don't know. Bull said — '

'Bull wants it this way,' Dutton said. 'Bring her out.'

Troon hesitated a moment, then shrugged. Dutton and the sheriff being here together didn't make much sense but what did he know? Bull had said to shoot anybody who came to take her other than himself but that obviously didn't include his son. 'Terry, fetch her out.'

Half a minute later Terry Miller brought her out. She looked weary and bedraggled but essentially unhurt. She looked at Ryder wide-eyed, but said nothing. He did likewise letting Dutton do all the talking.

'Hi, Amanda,' Dutton said.

She gave him a glance of pure hatred.

'Get up behind the sheriff,' Dutton said unabashed. 'I'm staying here a while.'

Ryder had thought he might try that, in effect bartering her freedom for his own, and wondered what he would do if he did. Now he knew.

'Do as he says, Amanda,' Ryder said. 'We're going back to town.'

She started forward and maybe it would all have gone hunky-dory if Terry Miller hadn't chosen that moment to notice that Dutton's ankles were tied together under the belly of his horse.

'Hey, Troon, it's a set up!' Even as he yelled he was grabbing for Amanda with one hand and drawing with the other.

Ryder, doing just one job, was a fraction quicker. He drew and fired. It was the duty gun from the sheriff's office and he still wasn't all that quick with it but once drawn he hadn't hesitated a moment and the boy had. It cost him his life for the heavy bullet caught him in the chest and sent him crashing down onto the rotting stoop of the sod house.

'Down Amanda!' Ryder yelled, and he hadn't commanded a troop of cavalry without acquiring the knack of command. She fell forward instantly. Troon's shotgun blast tore the air just above her.

The oldster was following orders — kill the girl first.

The horses shied at the shotgun blast so that Ryder couldn't get a clear shot at Troon as he was frantically reloading the Greener. Ryder reacted instantly, touched spurs to his horse's flanks, side-swiping Dutton's horse, intending to get it to move forward on the oldster. But it reared up instead and then took off, leaving Ryder and the oldster with nothing between them. Ryder saw his eyes, bright and resolute just like the Reb infantry when they struck them on the flank. Troon had reloaded his Greener now and the object of his aim was no longer Amanda — she could wait. The county sheriff couldn't. He was raising the gun to fire.

Ryder should have had the drop on him but he'd neglected to recock his Colt. He did so now and the click of the mechanism unaccountably set his horse shying then it raised its front hooves and though they were nowhere near the old cowboy he held fire and stepped back. Even if he'd only got the horse it might have given him enough time to reload again. Maybe he liked horses or just didn't think a man could fire accurately from a half-bucking horse. But Ryder was an old cavalryman and was used to firing at men with rifles and long guns whatever his own horse was doing.

The first shot took the oldster in the leg, spinning him back against the sod wall, but he still held on to the Greener.

Ryder cocked automatically now, fired again and then again until the hogleg clicked on empty, the oldster jerking against the wall under the impact of the heavy bullets like the marionette of a drunken puppet master.

7

Dutton Mazer was dead. Ryder found the horse just fifty yards off, Dutton lying battered on the ground, his legs twisted under the horse's belly, his neck broken — a hangman's break. Dutton hadn't quite cheated the rope after all.

Not that Ryder cared. He needed the horse for Amanda, he couldn't spend time looking around for where Troon and Miller had kept theirs. He cut the rope, heaved the dead-weight over the saddle and led the animal back to the sod house. There, he manhandled him off the saddle and into the house to join the other two. There was no point in advertising what had happened.

Inside, the rooms were stark and stinking; they had a kind of animal earthiness, dank and dry at the same time. The stink would be different soon enough but that would be for the undertaker to put up with. He went back out, closing the door behind him.

Amanda was sitting on the stoop where he'd left her. He went to her and sat down beside her.

'We can get back to town now,' he said gently.

She didn't reply, just sat there. He'd already asked the obvious questions and then she'd answered easily enough. She was fine, they hadn't hurt or insulted her. And it was obviously true, but now she was frozen somehow. Heck, she'd seen her father killed — or on the way to it — and just now she'd seen death dealt out quicker than a pack of cards and hardly less casually. He doubted too that she realized how lucky they'd been — getting the kid had always been on the cards but killing the oldster with the Greener had been pure good fortune — no, not quite. Using Dutton had made the difference and that hadn't been luck . . .

He reached out and pulled her to him. Suddenly her arms were about him and she was weeping.

'Let it out,' he said. 'Tears are good. Let it all out.' It was good advice too, for others.

★   ★   ★

They rode their tired horses through the night, stirrup to stirrup, and she saw him keep peering into that same dark looking out for Bull Mazer and his men. She wasn't worried. Cowboys rarely rode at night save when they were patrolling a herd. They were safe. And she was immensely grateful he hadn't suggested they stay at the sod house a moment longer; even before the killing it had been a place of horror to her.

Finally, emboldened by the protective night, she got up the courage to speak:

'I know I was going to die in that horrible place,' she began.

'It's over now,' Ryder said.

'But he's still alive — Bull Mazer,' she said. 'You've never met him, have you? If you had — '

'He's finished,' Ryder said, 'don't worry about him.'

'But you're going to arrest him and he'll — '

'Leave him to me,' Ryder said. 'I promise you, he'll not trouble you again.'

She said nothing. She wasn't afraid for herself, she was afraid for him. But she knew that nothing in the world would stop him from dealing with Bull Mazer now. She knew him too well to believe otherwise. The way he'd dealt with the three of them back there ought to at least calm her fears but it didn't. There was always a chance . . . and Bull Mazer was worse than he could imagine. She'd always thought him an ogre but seeing him standing before the barn, firing into it, urging his men to burn and kill was something she'd never forget. He was an ogre and more and Jack Ryder still had to face him.

Don't let him kill you, she prayed silently. I couldn't bear that and stay here . . . But those were words that could never be said aloud.

She found she was weeping silently, the tears rolling down her still begrimed cheeks, and she was suddenly grateful for the cloak of night.

Part Seven

1

Ryder watched them disembarking from the train. Some of them were wearing work clothes, others wore cheap suits, but Ryder had no doubt as to their true nature. They were soldiers. Not currently serving ones but only a few years ago virtually everyone of them would have been wearing blue or grey and now the difference didn't matter at all.

'I don't like this,' Bridger said, standing beside him, fully ambulatory now and leaning on his stick more out of habit then necessity. 'They're hoodlums.'

'Railroad detectives,' Ryder said, not totally in disagreement. He'd no doubt there were hard cases among them or maybe they all were, but he'd just had dealings with two of the weaker members of Bull Mazer's ranch hands and for all they'd ended up dead, they'd impressed him. They'd fought it out.

The first thing he'd learned as an officer was not to give any order until he was sure it would be obeyed. The second had been to ensure that it could be obeyed. A posse of store clerks and saloon keepers failed on both counts. And that was why he'd telegraphed Judge Shaw for armed assistance.

'Hell, they scare me,' Bridger added.

'That's the point,' Ryder said.

Bridger sighed. 'You came out here to be a lawyer, Jack. Now see what we've talked you into.'

'It needed doing,' Ryder said.

'Using the law,' Bridger said.

'In the end, that's what the law is,' Ryder said. 'Force. Hard cases with guns, wearing uniforms or badges or stars, but above all armed and willing to fight.'

'Judge Colt's six statutes?'

Ryder ignored him. He'd just seen Shaw dismount from the boxcar along with a tall man in a good suit wearing a gold badge pinned on his lapel. Ryder raised a hand. He could join them but Bridger had better be in on it too.

The pair cut through the milling detectives with an ease, which Ryder guessed was more down to the tall man with the railroad badge than the state judge.

Shaw shook his hand. 'Good to see you, Jack. What do you think of 'em?'

'They'll do.'

'Whatever's needed,' the tall man said.

'This is Lt Jones of the railroad police,' Shaw said.

Ryder accepted the lieutenant's hand. 'Welcome to Tamar County, Lt Jones.'

'Glad to be here, Sheriff Ryder.' He looked to Shaw. 'I've some unloading to do, Judge, if you'll excuse me.'

'Everything is up to the sheriff now,' Shaw said. 'It's his county, after all.'

'Winchesters?' Ryder asked.

'Plus four Springfields. It pays not to be out-ranged.'

Ryder nodded. 'Just get them all to

the court house in half an hour. The detectives will have to be sworn in as special deputies.'

Jones looked surprised. 'Is that necessary? They've all got railroad police badges.'

Bridger chose that moment to put in his two pennyworth. 'Think of it like baptism, lieutenant. It can't hurt and might help.'

Jones smiled grimly. 'You might just have something there, sir.' He turned and left.

'Let's get there first,' Shaw said. 'I've a warrant to sign and I'd better hear Amanda Thornton's complaint first.'

'She's with Mrs Cowper, the minister's wife, resting,' Ryder said. 'I've a deposition from her. It's at the court house.'

'It would be better if — '

'As I said, she's resting up. Lately, people have been dying all around her and rather too often, judge.'

Shaw glanced at him, saw he'd brook no argument. 'It's your county, Jack. Let's get to court.'

2

'Cannae!' Jones said later in the hotel when Ryder told him of his plan.

'What are you talking about?' Ryder asked.

'The battle, the one during the Punic Wars when Hannibal surrounded the Romans.' He smiled, slightly apologetically. 'It's my hobby you might say — military history.'

As they talked Ryder learnt that Jones had been conscripted but served out the war as a clerk corporal in a New York quartermaster's depot. He'd volunteered for more active service but his commanding officer hadn't cared to spare him. After the war he'd come out west in search of excitement.

'There's not much of it about any longer,' he confided. 'No Indians to speak of, and not much in the way of train robbery either.'

'We'll do our best to accommodate you,' Ryder said, smiling to himself, remembering his first battle. He'd been taught military history professionally but actual war and the schoolroom were miles apart. The little block diagrams of the books and the reality of men trying to kill you bore no relation to each other.

'What about your men, are they veterans?' Ryder asked.

'Rebs the lot of 'em,' Jones said. 'The company recruits in Georgia and the Carolinas on two year contracts. They pay less there.'

But they preferred the officer to have worn blue, Ryder noted silently.

'They'll fight well enough,' Jones said, suddenly defending his men.

Ryder believed him. At the swearing in they'd been in obvious high spirits and each carried a Winchester and a hundred rounds of ammunition. Together they had more firepower than a wartime battalion armed with caplock rifles. They'd do, and more than that, he knew now they'd do what he told them. He'd wondered when they arrived if Jones might try to take over but he was sure now that wouldn't happen. Cannae! They were here to surround a house, not eighty thousand Romans.

'What about the terrain?' Jones asked.

'It's flat,' Ryder said. He'd scouted the land on the same day he'd telegraphed Judge Shaw, not getting too close, but there'd been nothing to see. Just a big house and barn on a plain flat enough for playing bowls. 'We put a rig in front and one in back. The rest act as infantry and fill out the circle, going in as close as a hundred yards. Lying down nobody in the house'll hit them but they'll hit the house.'

Jones nodded. 'We can manage that.' He paused. 'Maybe they'll just give up.'

'Maybe,' Ryder said. Come to think of it, the encirclement was just a bit like Cannae. Except they weren't Carthaginians and sure as shooting the men in the ranch house weren't Romans. But the principle was the same. He only hoped the outcome was too.

★   ★   ★

It began without incident. They saw a pair of horsemen a mile out from the ranch house but they wheeled away and back. Nobody pursued them. The little army moved inexorably on, only halting when they were half a mile off the ranch house, itself nothing special, just a large balloon house constructed almost entirely of two by fours on a wooden frame.

Ryder detached off the second wagon to behind the house, wheeling wide and moving in; the riders he had dismount and take up their close positions. No one demurred. The ex-Rebs knew their business — cavalry was useless in attacking buildings, but lying flat with a Winchester a hundred yards off they had nothing to fear. He concluded his orders:

'We don't shoot first. But if they shoot first, we shoot last.'

That elicited a few grim smiles.

★　★　★

The encirclement was effected without opposition. They saw faces at the windows, the glint of gun barrels, but no shot was fired. The remaining wagon was taken in to one hundred and fifty yards off and then the horses were unhitched and led back, only he and Jones keeping horsed, the pair of them well protected in the lee of the wagon. As ordered, the other wagon was soon in place, not diametrically opposite though: three hundred yards would be a long shoot for a Winchester but odd things did happen.

'Shouldn't we send someone to ask them to surrender?' Jones asked.

'They're all wanted for multiple murder and arson,' Ryder said. 'At best they're looking at twenty years in state prison, but most of them will get the rope. Maybe they'll respect a white flag but I wouldn't care to bet my life on it. But if you feel inclined, you're welcome to try.'

Jones laughed, then: 'So what do we do?'

'We wait for their surrender. We'll respect their white flag.'

But none came, and no shots either. Ryder was well satisfied with his men, Rebs or not. They kept their positions patiently. He and Jones were now standing beside their horses, keeping them as fresh as possible. It hadn't been necessary to tell men not to lie in the wagon, Ryder noted. They were on the ground under and about it — one thickness of board might or might not stop a bullet at this range and a wagon is a big target.

'What are they doing in there?' Jones asked.

'They're arguing about what to do,' Ryder replied. 'Sooner or later they'll decide — surrender or shoot.'

'What would you do?'

'I'd wait for dark and break out. But that's hours off and they already feel the hemp around their necks. I reckon they'll shoot it out.'

'It's not like books,' Jones said. 'I feel — '

But at that moment the first shot came from the house and the reply of the railroad detectives followed a moment later. Ryder tied the reins of the horses to the wheel of the wagon, took the Winchesters from their sheaths and handed one to Jones.

'Don't feel,' he said, 'fire.'

3

Jones found his first battle nothing like he'd anticipated. He'd been about to tell Ryder he was feeling exhilaration but it would have been a lie. In all truth he'd felt simply impatient. Now, lying down and firing the Winchester at the wooden house he felt nothing much at all, save uncomfortable. The Winchester was awkward to fire prone thanks to its lever mechanism but you could manage by doing it sideways.

The 'battle' wasn't one continuous fusillade as he'd anticipated. There were bursts of firing, then silences, sometimes punctuated by a single shot, and then another flurry. There were no cries he could hear and nothing much to see except the powder smoke, not very thick, drifting across the beaten ground before them.

Occasionally a bullet hit the wagon or

the ground close by it but nothing really came close to him.

The whole experience, from feeding bullets into the magazine, to feeling the rifle press back against his shoulder as the heavy pistol bullet left the barrel, was out of time. It was as if he were not fighting men but a building, one he would remember forever in every external detail. Despite all the bullets expended, and he'd filled and fired off four magazines himself, the house seemed little affected. Even its broken windows had been broken from within.

Once he set down the rifle and took out his revolver, emptying that into the distant object of their strategic intentions, but Ryder snapped at him.

'You're wasting bullets. They won't carry.'

And he could see the sense of that. All the same it had been satisfying to blaze away without the interruption of the lever. He didn't reload or re-holster, just set the empty pistol beside him and returned to firing the carbine.

He lost count of the bullets he fired and even when one of the incoming bullets ricocheted off the tyre of the rig's outward facing back wheel and cut him in the hand, he paid it no attention.

Aim.

Fire.

Reload.

It was all there was, all there'd ever be . . . and then it ended.

The ranch house was on fire. Whether intentionally or by accident, one of the lower rooms was alight. Flames gushed out of the window, licking up the wooden wall and suddenly the whole house — ventilated by those broken windows — was ablaze, one vast sheet of flame.

He waited for figures to issue forth, even jumping from the upper windows, but none came. He could hear the fire now, a crackling and a whooshing sound like a thing alive and he realized time had returned to the battlefield and he was still alive and this was victory.

His hand started to hurt, paining him

like the devil, but he set the pain aside and stood up, aware that others were doing so too, and then he heard an even odder sound — the men were cheering.

It seemed wrong. Men didn't, shouldn't cheer at this and then he realized — they were Rebs still in their hearts and they had needed this, a tiny victory to balance a massive defeat.

He looked to Ryder who wasn't even smiling, just looking at the holocaust. The county sheriff noticed his glance, saw his hand. He pulled a kerchief from his pocket, came over to him and bound it round his hand. 'Have Doc Bluett look at that when we get back to town.'

He looked down at it, saw the red seeping through the white and looked away. Back at the fire. It was almost through. The flames had subsided and the blackened remains were writhing in the heat.

'Let's go and check the stables,' Ryder said and turned to the men now standing by the rig: 'Come on, let's hear you cheer when you see what's left of the horses.' And they went with him, Jones too.

But the horses, terrified though they were, were unhurt save for one which had a gashed flank, whether from bucking in the stall or from a bullet grazing it, it was hard to tell.

The barn itself seemed untouched, not a bullet hole to be seen for all it was near the house, but there was a smouldering smell to it that came from nearer than the blackened detritus of the house. Jones looked up and saw flickers of borrowed fire on the roof.

'Let's get them out of here!' he heard himself yelling and instantly men who minutes ago had been taking human life were now saving equine life at some risk to themselves, for no sooner had they got the horses into the open than that building too was ablaze, the fire starting at the top this time and pouring down over the walls like spilt whiskey down the side of a glass.

Jones joined Ryder as he walked over to the house, now a pile of ashes.

'What about the bodies?'

Ryder shrugged. 'The undertaker can see to that,' he said.

'But — '

Ryder turned to him. 'This isn't Cannae, nicely set out in some book by a chap who'd faint if he cut himself shaving.' He visibly caught hold of himself. 'It had to be done but I take no pleasure in it.' Suddenly he smiled. 'You did well, Lt Jones, and I'll say so. You won't get the purple heart for that hand but I'll make sure a letter of thanks goes to the directors of the railroad.'

Jones nodded his thanks, suddenly finding he didn't care all that much. He'd always wondered how he would have done on active service and now he knew — just like everyone else. But he hoped profoundly he'd never have to do anything like this again.

'Are we finished?' he asked.

'Unless you want to go chasing the hands out on the range.'

'They'll be in the next county by now if they've any sense.'

'And in another state by tomorrow. At least I would be.' Ryder paused, then: 'Justice has been served.'

Maybe that last was ironic, maybe not. Jones had caught a whiff of the smell from the house and it wasn't just burnt wood. He turned and walked back to the horses.

4

It was the first time Ryder had been in Mayor Jackman's house. It was the usual sort of frame house, of moderate dimensions, but inside he could just as easily have been in New York — the floors were carpeted, the furniture shining, the wallpaper an expensive print though mostly hidden by framed pictures; and every available ledge or table was covered with lace mats and bearing vases of much ornateness and colour. All this was presided over by a small, busy bee of a wife who cleared just enough space for them all — her husband, Judge Shaw, Lawyer Bridger and himself — to have somewhere to rest their coffee and cookies. She spoke only to ask Ryder how Miss Thornton was doing. Ryder noticed slightly amused expressions on the men's faces. Mrs Jackman hardly needed to ask in a town this size; she already knew. It was a form of ancillary matchmaking.

'She's doing fine, ma'am. I called on her again last evening.'

'She's a fine girl, poor dear, and no one to look after her now.'

'Yes, ma'am,' Ryder said, almost smiling himself. Then Mrs Jackman bustled out and left the men to their work.

'They've all gone?' Judge Shaw asked, picking up his coffee cup.

'Yes, the train left at noon. It was just as well as the saloon keepers had been giving out free liquor. They'd no love for Bull Mazer either but it wasn't a good idea. There was some talking of crowning their efforts by shooting up the town too — they were all former Rebs — but Jones and I dissuaded them.'

'Useful man, Jones,' Shaw said. It wasn't quite a question.

'He did well.'

'So now all our problems are solved thanks to you, Jack. The mayor can speak for the town but on behalf of — '

'Not quite, sir,' Ryder said. 'The shooting's over but Miss Thornton is without a father and her ranch is in ruins.'

'So's the Mazer spread,' the mayor put in.

'That's equitable in the broad sense but not at all in the legal sense, eh Jack?' Bridger smiled, a knowing look in his eye.

'Precisely.' He paused. 'It's never been said, at least to me, but let's get it said now — the whole of this business started with the need on the railroad's part to get a right of way through Mazer land. And Bull Mazer wasn't selling.' He looked to Shaw.

'That last's correct, anyway.'

'So a way had to be found to either kick him off the land or to get an agreement out of him. That's why I was brought in — not to do anything in that regard but to take the burden of work off Bridger here so he could work on just that.' He looked around, from one to the other, awaiting an answer.

'You've got the floor, Jack,' Bridger said.

Ryder took that as confirmation. 'But something unexpected happened. I offended Dutton Mazer, quite by chance, and half-mad as he was, he killed Sheriff Mason by mistake.'

'We know all this,' the mayor said, a little irritated.

'It's a lawyer's trick,' the judge said, smiling. 'Tell them first what they already know and only then what they don't. It inspires belief in the latter.'

'The latter's very simple, judge. By arresting Dutton Mazer I offended his father and he destroyed the Thornton spread. None of you had planned or even thought about that but it still suited your plans. He'd put himself outside the law. The state would now confiscate his estate and the railroad could buy its right of way without any problems.'

'We'll all profit by it,' Judge Shaw said, 'you included.'

'But Miss Thornton's ranch lies in

ruins, as I said.' He paused, briefly. 'As you know, I had a frank conversation with Dutton Mazer before he had his accident. I might have in my possession a document which he signed and in which he stated his father killed McIver and took the river land illegally.'

'Might?' Shaw asked sharply.

Ryder nodded. 'Just 'might'. I thought I'd better tell you that I'm leaving Mr Bridger's employ and am now acting exclusively on Miss Thornton's behalf and purely in her interests. It so happens she's contemplating a suit before the courts to gain compensation for the damage inflicted on the Thornton ranch. From the Mazer estate.'

'But that possible document of yours could complicate probate no end. It could be years before the land was free of litigation — '

'And the railroad got its extension,' Ryder interrupted. 'It's regrettable but then that line's not in my client's immediate interest, at least not at the moment.'

'And a long probate battle is?' Shaw asked.

'Naturally not. It might be expensive, she might well lose . . . but it would certainly take a very long time because I would of course appeal to the State Supreme Court.'

'And lose.'

'I won't argue law with you, judge. But in five years time will the railroad still be interested?'

'This is all damned ungrateful, Ryder,' Mayor Jackman put in.

'Hold your horses, mayor,' Shaw said. 'What's your offer, Jack?'

'She gets the whole of the Mazer spread in recompense for damage done to the Thornton spread.'

Bridger let out a breath. 'That's something!'

'It would cost you nothing, Stony,' Ryder said. 'Nor anyone here. And it is fair restitution. Added to which, as her lawyer, I'd strongly advise her to sell a right of way through the land to the railroad — either directly or to a cartel of interested parties.'

'For how much?' Shaw asked.

'Miss Thornton's in need of a float to put her ranch back on its feet. Mr Thornton died cash poor. Twenty thousand — '

'Ten thousand,' Shaw said. 'And the Mazer document?'

'You'd not want to see that now would you, judge?' Bridger put in.

'Nor would he have to,' Ryder said. 'There have been a lot of fires around here lately. It might have got burned up.'

'Agreed,' Shaw said suddenly. 'We can sort it out — '

'Why not now? The court's just across the street,' Ryder said. 'As for the agreement to sell a right of way, I'm sure the mayor can provide pen and paper. Either cash or a cashier's cheque will serve for payment for it.'

'I nursed a viper to my bosom!' Bridger said, almost laughing.

Judge Shaw only said, 'The court will open for business — '

He was interrupted by urgent rapping on the inner door. Mayor Jackman got to his feet and walked over to it, had a brief conversation with his wife and then went as near to the window as the excess of furniture allowed. He looked out down Main Street. A moment later he said:

'You'd better come and look, Sheriff Ryder.'

Ryder did and saw a very large man standing in the middle of Main Street. He didn't know him but felt he should. Then the other two came and looked out too.

Judge Shaw laughed nervously. 'I rather think the deal's off, at least for now.'

Ryder turned to face him but it was Stoney Bridger who spoke:

'That's Bull Mazer.' He paused, adding unnecessarily, 'He can't have been in the ranch house after all.'

'So why's he here now?' the mayor asked nervously. 'What's he come for?'

'For me,' Ryder said, extricating himself from the little crowd about the window and making for the door and Main Street.

5

Bull Mazer had come to Tamar City to die — but not alone. Everything was gone — his home, his ranch, even his horses were gone, lost forever.

He had killed twelve men in getting and keeping that ranch, in building it up from just four sections of semi-desert and two hundred scrub cattle to what had become — what had been — the greatest ranch in the region. He'd even been shot twice himself in the course of getting it together . . . all for nothing.

Dutton was dead. The boy had had his faults but he was still his seed, no doubt of that, and he would have kept the Mazer name alive, been his grip on eternity. But they'd taken him too.

So the Mazer name would have to be made permanent another way — by blotting out those who had done this to him. First the sheriff, the fancy eastern lawyer with soft words and hard hands, and then the fat man, Bridger, and Judge Shaw if he was about.

Maybe he'd not work his way all down the list but half way would do. Ryder alone would do. And the hard case railroad police were gone — he'd watched the railroad depot so he knew — and that meant he'd have a chance. He wasn't at all worried about what aid Ryder might try to whip up in town. They were a gutless lot in Tamar City.

But he was tired. Which was why he stood in Main Street and waited. Let them come to him. And now one was, a tall man in a dark suit, the sheriff. Good. Once he'd killed him, then he'd go for the gutless lawyers.

Just maybe if he killed enough of them he could put things back together . . . He put such nonsense out of his mind. Only the coming fight mattered now though he found himself regretting he hadn't killed those two gutless hands he'd had with him out on the range.

Once they'd seen the fire and the numbers against them, they'd taken off like the sandless scum they were. If they'd stuck by him at least he'd have somebody to guard his back, a real chance of getting them all.

He started walking towards the tall man. You win a fight by being aggressive, not by standing back. And suddenly the depression and the misery fell away from him. This was what he had always been good at — killing. And the odds were even. Everything was in his own hands now.

★   ★   ★

He was a bear, not a bull, Ryder thought. An old one too, huge boned and strong, the face set in a perennial scowl. Cruel and vicious but in a way admirable too, at a distance.

And the distance was growing less. He shouted:

'Throw down your gun and surrender!' pulling back his coat as he did so to reveal the star on his chest.

Bull Mazer didn't deign to reply except by drawing his gun and cocking it, and Ryder suddenly realized that if he stood up and exchanged shots with this mountain of a man he might well kill him but not before he'd taken several bullets himself. Old bears are hard to kill . . . and very slow to die.

Drawing his Colt he dived forward into the dust of the street, cocking and firing it from there, nothing fancy, just emptying all six cylinders into the torso of the big man.

Bull Mazer should have been knocked flat by the impact of even two of the bullets but amazingly he absorbed the multiple impacts as if they were tossed pebbles. He even got off one shot himself, but it was way off.

Finally, he fell. He didn't crash down. First he went to his knees and then slowly leaned forward, his massive arms holding him up, his head still level.

'I'll kill you — ' he began and then the dark eyes glazed over and he toppled forward and lay there like a fallen statue, the gun still in the massive, lifeless hand, jammed between it and the dust of the street.

Ryder got slowly to his feet. He was utterly drained but at the same time, he felt strangely exultant: as if he'd faced down death itself and won a unique victory.

He glanced at the empty gun still in his hand and felt a sudden repugnance for it. He let it slip from his fingers to lie in the street only feet away from the fallen giant.

Epilogue

In the illustrated dime novels a cattle barony always had a gate, usually a rustic-style triumphal arch, mostly topped off with cattle skulls or simply a set of the great long horns themselves. This was just a sign:

MASON CATTLE COMPANY

Ryder got out of the buggy, took hold of the post holding it, heaved it out of the ground and cast the whole down.

'Did you need to do that?' Amanda asked from the buggy.

'The Mason spread no longer exists as a separate entity. It's part of the Thornton spread now — from the desert to the mountains.'

Amanda frowned slightly. Why did he have to insist on the 'Thornton' spread? But she said nothing. She knew he had a right to be proud of what he'd done. She wasn't much up on legalities but she knew he'd taken on Shaw, Bridger and Jackman and beaten them at their own game, that he'd been surrounded by petty corruption and come through unscathed and untouched.

More than that, he'd killed that ogre Bull Mazer and then given her back her patrimony tripled, even buying the Mason spread off Deputy Gill for eight thousand dollars, thereby giving the new cattle company a ranch house and barn to work it from. She ought to be grateful but he would insist on calling it the 'Thornton' range.

Yet she daren't scold him. She was too conscious of her unflattering plain black dress, or her red rimmed eyes and the fact that no matter how often she bathed she still felt as if she smelt of the fire and that the stink of the sod house still hadn't quite left her.

She knew the biddies of the town speculated on whether or not she was 'shop-soiled' goods, maybe Jack did too.

Maybe he'd built up the Thornton spread into a little empire so he could feel free to leave her. Why not? What he'd done once he could do again. He didn't need her. But she needed him. Better to have been left in that filthy sod house on the prairie than to be abandoned now. And suddenly she was weeping, silently.

★   ★   ★

Ryder hesitated. It was a big step. He was free now, from the pain that had dogged him these last few years and from the law too, which had always been a second best anyway. Yet being a rancher wasn't at all what he had counted on. But Amanda was sitting there weeping . . .

He recalled something he had to do, reached into his pocket and brought out the power of attorney she had given him when he took her to the Cowper house. He'd used the first piece of paper to hand — the reverse was blank

214

save for a scrawled signature, Dutton Mazer's. He could have hung him with it, or filled it out differently and brought the railroad's plans down about their ears. But now it was just an empty flimsy with a scrawl at its base, one he had promised to destroy anyway. He tore it up.

'What are you doing?' she asked, wiping her eyes. 'I signed that. You said — '

'It's all right,' he told her. He couldn't tell her that her power of attorney had also been a potential death warrant, nor exactly how he had obtained it in the first place. He even wanted to forget that particular ploy himself.

'It's no longer needed,' he said. 'Or at least it won't be if I turn the buggy around and we take the noon train to the state capital. They have a justice of the peace there, I believe.'

And suddenly his freedom was gone and he knew that it had been illusory anyway. His true freedom was sitting up there in the buggy, her expression changing from misery to joy. 'And dress shops too,' he added, 'unless you want to marry in black.'

She didn't. But when they finally drove back towards town she said quite firmly: 'We'll want a new brand. We can order a dozen there. The Ryder brand.'

'Yes, ma'am,' he said contentedly and urged on the horse. They had a train to catch.

We do hope that you have enjoyed reading this large print book.

Did you know that all of our titles are available for purchase?

We publish a wide range of high quality large print books including:
Romances, Mysteries, Classics
General Fiction
Non Fiction and Westerns

Special interest titles available in large print are:
The Little Oxford Dictionary
Music Book, Song Book
Hymn Book, Service Book

Also available from us courtesy of Oxford University Press:
Young Readers' Dictionary
(large print edition)
Young Readers' Thesaurus
(large print edition)

For further information or a free brochure, please contact us at:
Ulverscroft Large Print Books Ltd.,
The Green, Bradgate Road, Anstey,
Leicester, LE7 7FU, England.
Tel: (00 44) **0116 236 4325**
Fax: (00 44) **0116 234 0205**

Other titles in the
Linford Western Library:

THE HIGH COUNTRY YANKEE

Elliot Conway

Joel Garretson quit his job as Chief of Scouts to travel to Texas and claim his piece of land. He needed to forget the killings he had seen — and done — fighting the Sioux and the Crow in Montana . . . But he soon has to confront Texas *pistoleros* and then, aided by a bunch of ex-Missouri brush boys, he faces the task of rescuing two women held by *comancheros* in their stronghold . . . In the territory of the Llana Estacado, New Mexico, the violent blood-letting will commence . . .